Discoveries
short stories

D1826013

John Wickham

LONGMAN

Longman Group UK Limited,
Longman House, Burnt Mill, Harlow,
Essex CM20 2JE, England
and Associated Companies throughout the world

Carlong Publishers (Caribbean) Limited
PO Box 489
33 Second Street
Newport West
Kingston 13
Jamaica

Longman Trinidad Limited
Boundary Road
San Juan
Trinidad

First published 1993

Set in 11/12 Baskerville

Produced by Longman Singapore Publishers (Pte) Ltd
Printed in Singapore

ISBN 0 582 21804 7

John Wickham is one of the most respected figures in Caribbean literature. Born and educated in Barbados, he has travelled widely in the Caribbean, Europe and North America. He worked with the World Meteorological Organisation in Geneva for four years and has represented Barbados and the Caribbean at meetings of the Commonwealth Conference of Arts Administrators. He was Chairman of the Canada-Caribbean Regional Panel of Judges for the Commonwealth Writers Prize in 1988 and 1989. He is the Editor of BIM, the Barbados Literary Magazine, and since 1979 has been Literary Editor of Barbados' *The Nation* newspaper.

A long established writer of short fiction, John Wickham's work has appeared in many magazines and anthologies. The style and concerns of his writing make it particularly suitable for school study and his work is often used by teachers, in Barbados and beyond, as a model of how to write and how to use the English language in ways that are both 'correct' and yet, also, distinctly Caribbean.

Previous publications include *Casuarina Row* and *World Without End*, both of which are collections of essays and short stories.

Foreword

The stories in this collection were written over a long period – more than forty years – in several places and environments. Naturally, most of them reflect in the essentials of their main characters the author's observations and perceptions of real people he knew to some degree. Some of them have a background of Barbados as is probably only natural, since this small island is where the author was born and grew up, and where the urge to write showed itself. Some of them, however, are purely fictional, made up out of ideas with the characters created to fit, rather than the other way round. *Galvan and Calliana*, for instance, was written as an entry for a competition in Trinidad and has no counterpart in real life.

But all the stories were spontaneous: none was designed to fit into any conscious pattern, none made to measure. However, when they were being put together, it became clear that all of them were the product of a response to one environment or another. Thus, discovery is a common feature of the stories.

There is an odd thing, another discovery, that although the events of each story, except perhaps *Galvan and Calliana*, take place in a more or less familiar setting or against a familiar background, yet each, when written and read, seems to reveal something about its place which the author did not know before the writing – which says something about the power of stories to generate their own energy and life.

The earliest of the stories – *Blood Brothers, Call it a Long Farewell, The Blue Dress, Christmas is for Children* and *Theresa* – come out of a Barbados experience and were published in BIM Magazine in the fifties. A certain chafing against the constrictions of a small island society and perhaps an anxiety to get away from it are recognisable. It was during this period that there was an exodus of West Indians to Britain.

The later stories, written when the author was away from Barbados are perhaps less resentful in tone; they reflect a backward glance at the environment of youth, perhaps a nostalgia. A kinder, gentler sentiment, for characters and landscape are noticeable features of these stories – *Casuarina Row, Septimus, Meeting in Milkmarket, Prospect, All of which Past, Till we meet in the Morning, The Light on the Sea* and *Alleluia Morning*.

This group may include *The Old Man and the City* and *Lunch Hour*, which are products of the author's Trinidad experience, while *Sorry, Wrong Jungle* is clearly born in London.

If a personal choice is permissible, the author would give his vote for *Lunch Hour, Meeting in Milkmarket, The Old Man and the City* and *The Light on the Sea*. These four stories have given the most pleasure to write, and to read over and over.

John Wickham
January 1993

For Grandson Ché and his generation,
in hope.

Contents

Lunch Hour

The girl came out of the dark dungeon of the shop and stood in the doorway smoothing the wrinkles out of her skirt. She looked to the right, to the left, rubbed her eyes against the sharpness of the light. After a pause, she stepped from the shop door and slipped unobtrusively into the tide of traffic moving along the pavement.

She had a lithe, slim figure but she was not tall. Her ankles were slender, strong-looking. She wore her hair parted in the middle, pulled back tight from her forehead and tied in a little bun at the back of her head. Her clothes were not dirty but they were not smart and carried a suggestion of patches in the unseen places. Her bright red skirt was shiny and her white blouse, although it was not nylon, had a transparency that exposed the broken, mended straps of her brassiere. At each stride her shoes showed worn soles and she walked quickly. The pavement was fire hot in the middle of the July day. Yet for all her quick walking she gave no appearance of haste for she did not swing her arms with her stride but held them close to her sides so that her gait was slinking and furtive like a cat's. Her face, if it had been white, would have been pallid. As it was, it was insensitive, somehow not quite alive. Her stare was dull and with her mouth half open she had a certain idiot vacancy of expression.

A group of boys in bright coloured socks and ready-made bow ties stood idly at the street corner leaning against the wall of the big grocery eating popcorn and whistling calypso tunes and jeering. With their sharp features and alert faces they were like rats nibbling the popcorn. She did not look at them as she passed under

1

their noses, smelling their body smells, sweat and Limacol and hair grease and the new leather of their fancy brass-buckled shoes. They did not see her, or if they did, did not care but went on whistling and buckling their shoes.

Six she-goats, all brown, wandered slowly, casually across the street picking at pieces of paper and refuse. All their bellies were heavy with young and their udders nearly touched the ground. The traffic stopped for them but they did not hurry. They were like matronly ladies, aristocratic and careless, knowing that in their delicate condition people would be kind and forbearing. Their udders swung from side to side like pendulums when they walked.

The girl went up the street and through the square where the ground was cool, cooler to the soles than the pavement and she could walk slowly. When she stopped hurrying her face slowly lost its lack of expression but it was not easy to tell exactly how.

In the sun a dog lay stretched out motionless near the fountain, as motionless as the corpse of a dog. A mangy derelict of a dog, starved to the bare ridges of its ribs. People walked on either side of the stretched out body, evading it, pretending not to see it, thinking whatever thoughts they were capable of, remembering whatever of their youths and pasts the sight of a brown dog lying in the sun near an idle fountain could evoke, but never pausing, never looking back.

The people in the square moved flatly, more like two-dimensional cardboard figures than like real people. A tourist couple took pictures of each other. She stuck a bougainvillea flower in her hair and leaned against a flamboyant. He adjusted the camera, measured the distance, inspected the light. They laughed together, having fun. The girl went through the north gate and up the library steps. She turned and paused for a moment, looking through the tracery of the fabric, pale honey-coloured in the sunlight and the sprawling red mass of the Government offices. There were very few sounds and those few were muffled: the noon heat had reduced even sound to unreality. Suddenly the church clock chimed the quarter but the chimes were muffled too, coming from far away. She turned, sighed a little and went through the library door.

The reading room was very still, almost empty. The attendant sat in her chair looking across rows of books, her thoughts far from books. At the table behind the mayor's bust, the chair was empty. The girl picked up two magazines and went into the far corner and settled herself in the chair. How still it was! Only the sound of the clock on the wall disturbed ever so faintly the heavy, motionless air. How time went on and on, never stopping when you were sixteen, when you were sixty! What then was the difference between sixteen and sixty? Some wrinkles? What else? Would she ever be sixty? Oh, what was the use? She was sleepy and hungry.

She had tried hard but she could not stretch her five dollars a week to Friday's lunch, not after she had taken out her busfare and the shilling for Grandpa's weekly ration of tobacco. Walking home after work might have done it, but the walking merely sharpened her appetite and left her dissatisfied with the evening cocoa. A little with contentment is great gain, so she had to take the bus. In the end she decided to do without Friday's lunch. Friday was pay day and the hollowness of her hunger was dispelled, or nearly, by the thought that at five o'clock she would get her pay. She pretended that she preferred to read on Friday and the time passed quickly.

The place was deathly quiet. Not a sound. Across the square, not the stir of a branch nor the movement of a leaf. The first showerdrops fell, a sweet rippling sound on the roof. She felt cosy and comfortable inside the building, out of the rain, dry. But she was very tired and sleepy. And hungry . . . In other buildings, other people were settling themselves in chairs, picking up knives and

3

forks and spoons, eyeing filled plates, choosing mouthfuls, shovelling pieces of meat and lumps of curried potato and rice down their eager, salivating mouths, rolling the sweet seasoned taste of fresh fried crisp brown fish around their tongues, smelling, while they chewed, the flavour of onion and garlic and pepper, not sure, not caring whether they were tasting or smelling. In other buildings under roofs on which the falling rain beat gently, sleepily, people were eating food. God! People were eating . . . chilled slices of Julie mango flavoured with Angostura and sprinkled with grated nutmeg, thick split pea soup, creamy peas boiled to pulp, fresh steamed fish garlanded with onions, chicken, stuffed and baked brown all over . . . people were eating and fat men were patting their bellies and belching and washing the food down with long glasses of cold beer and crossing themselves, saying for such as we have received may the Lord make us truly thankful, and pushing back their chairs and smiling . . . The rain fell soothingly on the roof, soothingly and so far away that she could barely hear it, a faint swish-swish-like wind in trees distantly, like the rustle of a taffeta skirt at a dance, but soft, sibilant, whispering.

The rain stopped suddenly and the sky seen through the trees was blue and clean. High overhead, a pair of corbeaux, their ugly black hideousness too far away for revulsion, wheeled and soared and floated; wing to wing they rose and fell, dark shapes sharply etched against the new washed sky, free as air.

The girl walked through the square. Every now and then, a little wind would shake the trees and the raindrops would fall bucket-a-drop. Inside her shoes her feet were wet now and she walked quickly. A raindrop glistened on a hibiscus leaf, emerald green one moment, ice blue the next, then gold in the sunlight. She stopped to see what new colour it would take, but a little wind came and it fell and was lost. She started to walk quickly again. All the people were walking quickly. A bird's note sounded shrill and clear and lonely. The sound hung in the air, almost visible before it fell and died away. But she did not check her quick stride.

At the corner of the square, a young man doffed his hat and smiled. His teeth were as white as milk, and from his high cheekbones the laughing lines ran deep beside the corners of his mouth. Fleeting as the smile was on his Semitic·arrogant face, she noticed the delicate volutions of his quivering nostrils. He had long fine hair on the back of his hand. She had never seen him before, but she felt a little surge of unknown, unsuspected feeling for him. But he was quickly past her, walking away. When she looked back, she saw only his back disappearing behind the fountain. The Assyrian came down like a wolf on the fold, she murmured, remembering Grandpa's warning when she went to work at the shop. And then she wondered. Why did I think that? I wish I knew him, he looked proud but perhaps he is kind.

The girl stepped off the pavement and crossed the street. Some of the shops on the eastern side of the street had already pulled their shades against the afternoon sun. No one stood now by the grocery corner, no one but a beggar with outstretched palm, empty. Dirty brown water flowed in the drains along the street. The traffic lights changed and the cars splashed the street people when they crossed the drain. Some raindrops drip-dripped off the eaves. One fell in her hair, chill, cold as ice, but refreshing. She put her hand to her head and smoothed her hair. With her hair parted in the middle and pulled back tight from her forehead, she was like a Madonna. She went across the street on her heels, for her feet were squirming inside her shoes, and in a moment she was lost in the darkness of the shop.

Beyond the grocery, high above the buildings, the church clock chimed the hour.

Christmas is for Children

December had come with its blue purity of sky, and the wind was rustling and bustling in the trees around the square. The cotton wool clouds tumbled across the sky in headlong, mysterious mirth. Timothy looked out from the window and sniffed the bouquet of Christmas in the early morning air. Down in the street below, the day's traffic was slowly beginning and in the room behind him, the radio blared out that there were only fifteen shopping days before Christmas.

Robert's voice came from under the blankets, muffled and heavy with sleep: 'Oh, turn that blasted radio off. Christmas! Nothing but Christmas, Christmas!'

Timothy paid no attention to him. Yesterday he had said that Christmas was only for children and now this morning he seemed in a worse mood than ever. Thinking it over, he realised that there was something in what Robert said. He himself had had the same feeling. Every year, he waited for something wonderful and extraordinary to happen at Christmas, and every year without fail, it turned out to be the same as any other day. He was tempted to believe that the whole thing was a fraud and a trickery. Still, he never succeeded in stifling the hope that surged every year when December came. If Christmas was for children as Robert said, then he and a lot of others, millions of others, were children. Perhaps everybody was a child.

Below, the street was busying itself as the shops opened and displayed their goods. There were toys in one shop window and extravagances of laces and ribbons and finery in another. The sweepstake ticket sellers were out early advertising the Christmas races with a little more gusto and cheerfulness than usual. Their hoarse cries, 'You ain't got a chance if you ain't got a ticket!' sounded, for once benevolent, as if they sincerely wanted to make everyone a present of thirty thousand dollars for Christmas. Even the beggars standing by the church wall in their attitudes of ragged patience seemed infected by the spirit that stalked abroad, and they looked brighter and more hopeful than usual. The radio in the room blared again that there were only 15 shopping days between now and the Day, and this time there was urgency in the announcer's voice. Christmas had moved a few minutes nearer.

Timothy could not deny the excitement he felt, and when he turned from the window, he felt, somehow, like a child again. He pulled his old suitcase from under the bed and began to pack.

From the road he could not see the old house. It had been such a long time since he had thought of the house as home, or indeed, had thought of it at all, that he began to wonder if it had not always been a sort of mirage, a figment of his own imagination. Nevertheless, he felt little needles of fear that the years might have destroyed the only home he ever knew, and, when he turned the corner by the sour grass hedgerow, and saw the old fashioned gables and the square brick chimney resisting the throttling efforts of the creepers and the foliage, he felt a wild exhilaration.

The driveway up to the house was overrun with weeds – a certain indication that Grandpa was no longer up and about. Everything seemed cast in a smaller mould than he could remember. The pillars under the verandah which had long ago been so easily identifiable with those which Samson had pulled down about the heads of the Philistines, seemed to his adult scrutiny the puniest, most pygmy pillars ever designed. The verandah itself, which had offered such unlimited area for 'jockey-and-horse', now confessed itself a narrow confinement, not wide enough for him to stretch out his legs. But still, it was the same house, standing as always on the top of the slight rise of the driveway and looking north to the hills and the railway line. The kitchen roof jutted out, as ever, from the back edge of the house, for all the world like an afterthought, as if they had built the house and then, suddenly remembering that people had to eat, had stuck on the kitchen at the last moment. He thought of it as a postscript to a rambling, ineffectual letter.

The whole house was aged beyond expectation, and decrepit like the worn out old age pensioners he sometimes saw in the warden's office, tired and wrinkled and frayed.

He spent a long time outside the house before he went in. Round by the backyard, the old hog-plum tree was rough-bearded as ever, but smaller than it seemed before. The back fence and the stable where Jimmy, the donkey, used to live: they seemed, too, to have 'grown down' with the years, and he could hardly believe that there had been a time when the fence had proved barely climbable.

There was no sound in the house when he pushed the side door of the veranda and went in. There was only a dim silence and an air of waiting. A massed array of memories bore down upon him. Grandma was sitting in the rocking chair near the old harmonium, rocking silently and sightlessly. As he entered, Grandma stopped rocking and waited.

'It's me,' he said, 'Timothy.'

'Timothy?' she asked, as if she had never heard the name. And then, 'Oh, Timothy, of course.' Grandma waited a little to grow accustomed to the thought, and then she said, 'Come and let me touch you, Timothy, and see if your ears still stick out!'

He walked across to the rocking chair, and stooped and kissed the soft wrinkled flesh on Grandma's face.

'I came to see you and Grandpa,' he said. His presence seemed to need some sort of explanation.

'I know,' Grandma said, 'you've come for Christmas. Grandpa's inside, asleep. He can hardly keep awake these days. Getting old, you know.' And she chuckled to herself. 'I'll go and look around the house, Grandma,' he said, but she did not seem to hear him. He turned away and left her wrapped in her own thoughts, rocking and chuckling to herself. Suddenly he was filled with an undiluted happiness.

The days to Christmas sped all too fast for him. There was much he had to do and to see. It was difficult to talk to Grandma and Grandpa; they both seemed to forget that he was grown up now and that he had left home long ago. They talked about things that had happened before he was born as if they had happened only yesterday, and they often forgot that he was in the house. They lived in only a small part of the house, and a woman came in the morning to do the little cooking and cleaning they needed. The rest of the house was deserted, and he spent the days wandering around and wallowing in a welter of memories.

In the cellar, he found the piece of white coral he had picked up one day on the beach. He saw the door of his room unhinged and remembered the night of the earthquake, how the glasses on the sideboard had jingled and tinkled together, and this selfsame door had swung and swayed as if a prankful ghost were swinging on it. The breadfruit tree reminded him of the many times he had bathed under it, naked in the rain. In the kitchen, the big stone where the wood was chopped was still lying on the floor near the dusty fireplace. He remembered that one of his ambitions had always been to grow big enough to move the stone. Now he tried, pushing it over easily on its side. A centipede, purple, almost black with age – the very grandfather of centipedes – disturbed and robbed of the warmth, slowly uncurled and slithered across the floor, seeking new shelter in one of the cracks in the

9

concrete floor. He watched it run away and felt almost sorry for having disturbed the old man's sleep and his own memories.

And so he passed the time to Christmas, the days speeding quickly and quietly away, spinning themselves out in a pattern of calmness and remembering.

Christmas, the day itself, dawned with a chatter of blackbirds in the mango tree. He pushed open the window and looked out at a sky innocent of cloud. Although there was no wind, it was cool and there was a glow in the east where the sun was rising. It was a morning for glory and jubilation and wild hosannas. He put on his trousers and tiptoed out of the house.

The grass was wet with dew when he pushed the back gate and stepped out into the old potato patch now overgrown with weeds and wild flowers. An instinct guided his footsteps and made a path for him through the pond grass, and urged him down the slope behind the sour-sop tree out towards the low wall Grandpa had built to keep out the water from the road. Suddenly he was struck by the familiarity of his actions and he had the feeling, unaccountable but real, that somehow, long ago, he had done the things he was doing now. He was dimly conscious of having, just so, pushed the back gate and stepped out into the wet grass on just such a morning as this, with no cloud and the glow of sunrise. Everything had a faint quality of rehearsal about it, a magic mixture of strangeness and familiarity. His feet were damp inside his shoes, and he jumped and sat on the low wall and swung his feet, feeling, as he did so, that he was fulfilling an already fulfilled destiny. He sat still and watched the sunrise, and waited, and waited . . .

There was no movement and there was no sound. Suddenly, as he seemed to expect, almost inevitably, the bean vines shivered on their trellises and the figure of a small girl moved towards him. Her feet were bare and glistened wetly with the dew off the grass. He felt a magic awareness of the moment like a sort of ecstasy, growing inside him – a bubble, a slowly swelling bubble that grew bigger and bigger, threatening to burst, as the girl moved closer towards him. It seemed that time was unfolding itself around him to a rhythm his consciousness recognised. It was magic, mystery; it was a miracle, but it did not seem wholly strange.

The figure moved closer, closer, until he could see a pair of liquid, tender eyes. His anxiety was urgent.

'Jacqueline!' he cried, at the instant of recognition.

Suddenly, the sun was splendid in the sky. The wind sprang up, rustling in the treetops, and the bean vines trembled on the trellis work. A chorus of blackbirds along the fence swelled into a crescendo of Christmas joy and the whole world came to life with hallelujahs of gladness and revelation. The house lay behind the trees, silent and remote. All at once, he felt like a child again and he was not surprised that there were tears in his eyes. Christmas was for children.

The Blue Dress

Julia put on her blue linen dress, the old one she had made for herself which Philip always said fitted her so well. Her mother wanted her to wear the red frock, the new off-the-shoulder one, because, she said, it was brighter and more of a dress for welcoming home a returning warrior.

'You ought to wear something bright and vivid,' her mother said, 'to remind Philip that he is back home in the West Indies; something like Carnival and calypsos and bright ixora flowers in the sunshine.' In her mother's view, blue was not a welcoming colour.

Julia's gladness for Philip's return after a long four years was a quiet gladness, like her blue linen dress, sober, without hilarity; but well-fitting, comfortable and becoming. But she couldn't expect her mother to understand that. She couldn't expect anybody to understand her attitude to the returning Philip.

In the hushed afternoon quiet of her room, Julia listened to the sounds of her mother, busying herself in the kitchen 'getting tea ready,' and the tinkle of china and silver made her think what a long time four years really was. More than a thousand days and a thousand nights. Long enough for her mother to forget that Philip was not the sort of person you offered tea in the afternoon. It was impossible for her to imagine the tall, handsome Philip she knew sitting in the drawing-room, sipping tea and making frivolous, genteel conversation and skirting the warm, full-blooded reality of himself and her. The idea was ridiculous. Philip did not fit into the pattern her mother was weaving. At least he used not to. But

perhaps he had changed. Four years was a long time,
and God knows what could happen to a person in that
long succession of days and nights in a strange place
and a bleak, alien climate. For all she knew, Philip
might well have adopted this strange habit of tea in
the afternoon. That was why she was wearing her blue
linen dress. Because she didn't know how things would
be. It was such a long time. Perhaps he had changed
altogether. True, his letters had never lacked warmth
and passion and he had written regularly, every week
nearly, but how could she be sure that face to face
with her he would be the same as he used to be?
Darling Philip! She found herself thinking out aloud
and she felt the grief-lump in her throat choking her
with sadness. How strange that she should be sad at
Philip's return! It was easier for her to accept the fact
that he was away and to live vicariously through his
letters than to face the reality of his return and the
chance of his having changed. Away from her he was
the real, the original Philip; returned, he might be a
stranger. But the blue dress would help to ease the
tension of their first meeting. He would notice that
she was wearing it and remember the days before he
went away. Long afternoons in the sun on Gravesend
beach, under the manchineel trees among the graves
of the old soldiers. He would remember, as she had
never forgotten, how the sea broke on the sand and
left a long, wavy line of seaweed along the shore, and
the surf foam coruscated in the sunlight. And perhaps
he would remember how he talked to her of the islands,
their islands, with their heritage of sun and sea and wind
that made them beautiful. Bright flowers in the ditches
along the country roads. White teeth and ebony black
skins of peasants in the fields and deep-bellied laughter
thrown insolently in heaven's face. He had made her see
that there was beauty instinct her land, before her eyes.
Sugar cane arrows waving in the wind; the electric blue

of October's lightning arrowing from the black, starless sky. Philip had made her call the names of the flowers and the trees and the places slowly; he had made her roll them over her tongue like a thick golden glob of syrup. Cassia, hung with the candleflies at night, poui and imortelle, flamboyant, frangipani, pink and white, whose bark, the old people said, would spout the rich red blood of Jesus if punctured at midday on Good Friday. The mile-long casuarina with the thin whisper, the poinsettia, the bougainvillea and the hibiscus, red as poppies on Armistice Day, and ginger lilies and lady-of-the night perfuming the gardens.

And there were the places on the islands he knew. The names rolled off his tongue richly until they were like the taste of wine to her. Chantimelle of the broken bridge, La Fillette on the hill where Augustus Welcome lived; Calivigny, separated by the sea, retreat for English millionaire recluses; Majuba Hill, where you walked with your lover at midnight if you wanted your love to last till death; Penny Hole, where the sun rose like shining copper out of the sea on Christmas morning; Fairy Valley, set between the hills and the sea, and Bathsheba, where the fishermen launched their boats, stark naked in the early morning, and where the parish priest held his matins by the water's edge; and Manzanilla, loveliest of names, and Grande Anse, miracle of white sand and blue water. Philip had even started a poem for her, but he had never got further than the first line – *In our land, too, there is beauty*. He had written the words with his finger in the rich brown-sugar sand, but they had lasted only until the next wave broke on the shore and washed them away, and now no one knew them but herself and Philip, and he might have forgotten.

There was beauty too in her body, he had said, in her bare brown legs and her lissomeness. But he had taught her that only through his letters, when he was far away from the reality; when, he said, the memory

14

of her brownness kept him alive and warm in a bleak, raw climate.

Julia was staring through the open window at the hedge where the crotons, a mass of brilliant reds and yellows and browns, glinted in the afternoon sun. Ginger was catching lizards under the hedge, and her tail waved slowly to and fro as she lay in wait. Everybody, thought Julia, waits for something: Ginger waits for lizards, I wait for Philip. The evening was still, and only the sound of 'tea-things' reached her from the kitchen. She hoped her mother wouldn't make herself look silly this afternoon. She had a habit of saying the obvious, and her idea of conversation was to ask a lot of questions and give a lot of opinions. Philip had understood her, in a way, before he went away, but he might not now. She would try to get him alone to herself and establish the old relationship before her mother got the chance to spoil everything.

She went into the drawing room and approved of it. Tidy, but not too obviously prepared for the hero's entrance. It had a pleasant air of being-always-so that Philip, the old Philip, would like. He wouldn't like to think that he was expected and prepared for.

'Oh, hello, Julia!' The strange voice at the front door made her start and she felt as if a stranger had intruded on her privacy. The tall upstanding figure framed in the door's light was a stranger to her. Only the slight tilt of the head and the blue uniform told her that Philip had come back.

'Oh, Philip!' she cried, and threw herself into his outstretched arms. He held her to him and kissed her on the forehead.

'Four years is a long time,' he said.

'Four years is a long time,' she said, in between her sobs.

Philip held her at arm's length and looked her all over. 'But you haven't changed a bit,' he said, 'you're just the same as you were when I left.'

She could not trust herself to speak, to ask him whether she should have changed. She kept silent. The evening ticked momentously away.

'Where's your mother?' he asked.

'She's in the kitchen, I'll call her.' And she ran out of the room, glad to escape for a moment to compose herself and dry her eyes.

They sat in the drawing room and drank tea, Philip, her mother and herself, sipping from the seldom used best china. Her mother had her little finger crooked the way that always infuriated her, but this evening she didn't care. Really, her mother was asking the most ridiculous questions. What is England like? Is it really as cold as they say? Is the food shortage really as bad as all that? Exactly what is a spiv? Philip gave her the answers she could have found in any newspaper and she was satisfied.

Julia watched Philip drinking tea and answering her mother's questions. Yes, he had changed. His voice had changed. He had lost the sing-song accent of the islands, at least most of it, and in its place there was a flatness of tone that displeased her. Why did he have to change his accent? In her mind she accused him of 'putting on'. Why, he himself had told her that there was beauty in it. Even angels have accents, he had said; what was there to be ashamed of? What indeed? She watched him bend over and help himself to another piece of cake from the tray and wondered at his stiffness. All the suppleness had gone out of his body: he was all angles now, no curves. Perhaps that was his military training; but in any case, he was a different person. She should have known that from the very moment he had accepted her mother's offer of tea with such pleasure. The old Philip would have laughed at the idea and shown his strong white teeth in amusement. 'Tea in the tropics?' he would have said. 'No, thank you.' And then he would have said, 'I'd prefer a rum.' That was the Philip she had known and loved. She could not recognise the formal-mannered man who smiled indulgently at her mother and answered her questions with only a suspicion of boredom in his face. She took no part in the conversation across the table. Can four years do this to a man? she asked herself. What was this England that could change the spark that was her Philip into such a paleness, such a nothing?

'Well, I think I'll run off and leave you young people to yourselves,' she heard her mother saying. She pulled herself together for the ordeal of rehabilitation. Her mother went through the door and she watched her close it softly behind her.

For a long time there was silence. She looked into Philip's eyes. They were the same hazel colour they always were. Eyes don't change, she thought. That's why they put down the colour of eyes on people's passports. Her thoughts wandered off.

'Well,' she heard Philip saying, 'tell me everything.' The voice was now faintly familiar and brought back the old Philip to her. Hope sprang up afresh and she looked down at her dress in the hope that he would follow her eyes and remember. And then . . .

'Everything?' she asked, when she felt that Philip was waiting for an answer and the silence had become unbearable.

'Yes, everything,' his voice came to her from far away. 'Four years is a long time.'

'Yes, I know,' she said, 'but you should tell me. You've been in the big world outside.' She tried to keep the sarcasm out of her voice, remembering that he had once told her, long ago, that he didn't believe in any world outside. It was all myth, he had said, there was no big world outside; these islands were the world, the real world; and when all the big cities of underground railways and gigantic buildings were nothing but heaps of ruins, hunting grounds for archaeologists, these islands would still be living, secure and remote, bathing in the sea and the sun, the original God-given paradise.

'I wouldn't have missed it for worlds,' he said. 'It was a wonderful experience.' And she knew then that the big world outside would always stand between them. She felt a sudden sense of loss and futility, and the shock of it made her desperate.

'Philip', she said, and she saw him look at her, startled by the new despair in her voice. 'Don't you remember . . .?' Her voice trailed off to nothing as she realised the futility of forcing the memory upon him. If he had forgotten, then let him forget!

'Remember what, Julia?' His voice had a formal tenderness in it.

'Oh, nothing,' she said, hiding behind the nothing.

'What is it, Julia? What's come over you?'

The tears welled up in her eyes and she felt the past swelling inside her, ready to burst.

'Don't you remember,' she asked him, 'how once we, the two of us, you and I, made a list of the things we loved, and you said I should keep it until you came back to see if you'd changed? Remember?'

'Oh, yes, I remember.'

'Do you, Philip?' she asked. 'Walking barefooted on warm sand was one of them. And crushing evergreen acorns under your feet, and bathing in the rain and the smell of the earth after rain; fish frying in the kitchen, raindrops winking in the potato leaves, men in the country singing hymns on Saturday nights, half drunk by the church corner; the hills by moonlight, the smell of cane fields during reaping, black pudding by the street corners, and cool rain. You called it the arithmetic of rain on the roof. Don't you remember, Philip?' She felt better now, relieved of her burden of memories.

'Yes, I remember,' Philip said, and smiled. 'But weren't we childish then?'

She did not answer.

'So much has happened since then.' The words of denial were a wound to her.

18

Julia looked down at the hem of her blue dress, the dress on which she had pinned so much faith, the talisman she was relying on to resurrect the Philip of long ago for her. It had failed. He hadn't even noticed she was wearing it. The room was silent and sunset-flooded.

'Yes, Philip,' she said at last, 'Four years is a long time.'

Blood Brothers

The sun was boiling hot and the house was stifling him, so Paul took his pencils and his water colours and went to sit under the casuarina trees. The air was still and it shimmered in the noonday heat and Paul felt sleepy, but he fought against the sleep; and, gripping the pencil in his fingers, set about the sketch he was about to make. The picture he wanted to paint he could see in his mind more clearly than with his eyes. For all of his thirteen years, he had seen the things he was seeing now and they were etched in his memory, an indestructible part of him, indivisible from himself and his own thoughts, a part of him that not even his twin brother Benjy and his insufferable complex of superiority could destroy. The long grass bent in the wind, the hibiscus flowers shone violent red in the sunlight and the casuarinas swayed and spoke in sibilant whispers. It was cool under the casuarinas and Paul stuck the pencil in his mouth and, lying flat on his back, looked up through the gossamer lacework of the trees' foliage to the sky.

Funny, thought Paul, that in the daylight casuarina trees could be so tall and graceful and slender and lovely, swaying in the wind and bending, whispering ever so languidly like lovely ladies in pictures; and yet at night, by starlight and moonlight, they assumed such fantastic, frightening, ghostlike shapes.

Casuarinas at night! Paul shuddered at the memory. He and Benjy had set out for a walk with their father after dinner one night. Paul remembered even now, after six or seven years, that the moon was rising when they left home and Benjy had been in even gayer spirits than usual; he had just discovered that he could whistle. Paul remembered too that Benjy's laugh had mocked him because he had not yet learned to whistle and he had been silent at this added proof of his brother's superiority. He hated Benjy for this small triumph and for his sneering contemptuous way of being able to do everything better than he; for treating him with his air of studied disdain, as if he were a little girl who had to be helped over fences, who wasn't expected to climb trees and bring down birds with catapults, and who would burst into tears for nothing that he, Benjy, could understand.

Paul remembered that, when they had turned into Garnet Road, the casuarina shadows were lying across the road in fantastic shapes, delicate shadow, diffuse in the soft light, weird and macabre; and the wind was whispering thinly through the trees with the unearthly voice of a ghost. The whole picture was faintly lit by the spectral light of the moon slanting through the trees, and he had been afraid. He had clutched his father's hand and his father had, it seemed, understood that he was afraid and had squeezed his hand in reassurance. Only Benjy, unaware and unafraid, hopped and danced along the road, exploiting his newly discovered whistle and flaunting his own complete lack of fear, his own blatant intrepidity in the face of the wraithlike shadows and the ghostly voices of the trees. As Paul pieced together the memory of long ago, his heart filled with a full-blooded hate for his blood brother.

Paul looked up through the trees at the sky and knew that in Benjy's eyes he was a coward. It was no solace to his wounded spirit to know that Benjy had never called him coward. His brother's own lack of fear, his recklessness and his arrant devil-may-care swagger was, to him, an unspoken insinuation of his own cowardice, and he felt the stigma of his own timidity each time Benjy and he played together, his self contempt and distaste for his own chicken-heartedness implicit in his slavish, albeit unwilling, hero worship of his twin brother.

Paul hated Benjy with a bitter passionate venom; and with all his heart's fierceness, he hated and despised himself for hating him. In quiet moments, as now, alone with himself staring up at the blue pool of the sky or sketching on the hill with the wind in his ears, it was easy for him to love his brother as himself. When he rose early in the morning and walked through the dew-wet grass to his spot on the hill, he wished that Benjy could be with him: he would like to talk to him, to tell him that he really wasn't a coward, that there were all sorts of queer little goings on inside him, that he knew the way of the blue mist on the green hills, the way of the white pigeons flying in joyous circles around the house. He yearned with every fibre of him, with a fervour not damped by these many years of vain wishing to share with Benjy the secret ways of his heart. He wanted to link arms with Benjy, to tap from his limitless reservoir of courage some measure of it for himself, so that the two of them could walk together as one. He yearned for this so deeply that he was afraid, afraid that Benjy, 'the little man,' so universally applauded for his daring, so consistent in his acts of heroism – climbing to the top of the tamarind tree careless whether he fell, daring to crawl under the house to search for the hens' eggs in the darkness, breaking his arm and betraying not so much as a wince when the doctor at the hospital set it – afraid that Benjy would reject his offer and interpret his overture as another proof of his cowardice. Paul hugged his secrets close and retired into himself, his thought buried so deep inside him that they turned sour and the germ of his potential love turned to bitter hate.

Sometimes, the violence of his hate frightened Paul and he trembled, unable to contain within his frail body the seething tumult of his inner conflict – the love he bore his brother, the admiration he had for his popularity and the twinkling smile in his eye contending in his heart with his own envy, the timid sense of his own timid spirit and his own tongue-tied shyness; and out of the turmoil inside him, there sprouted his own violent hate, deep and morbid because it was rooted and nurtured in the fertile compost heap of his own unavowed love. And always, Paul hated Benjy's presence for reminding him of the night of the ghostly shadows and the thin whisper of the casuarinas.

Benjy sauntered through the back gate, his teeth biting deep into a piece of bread. Paul guessed that he had rifled the larder; for Benjy, it seemed to him, would do that and glory in the doing. Benjy swaggered past Paul, lying on his back under the trees, in an exaggerated goose step of triumph, secure and unassailable in the citadel of his own good humour and blithe spirit, never dreaming that there could be anyone in the whole wide world who did not wish him well, and caring less than a row of pins for anyone who wished him evil. Paul's hate grew big. Look at him, he said to himself, strutting like a cock; he knows I'm watching him, he's only pretending that he doesn't care.

Benjy sat under the tamarind tree and finished his bread. When he had finished, he got up and began throwing stones idly across the pasture. He grew tired of this after a short while and Paul's eyes were on him when he tossed his head in defiance of the boredom that was setting in. He called out to Paul; 'see who can throw farthest!' he shouted.

'No,' Paul answered back. His voice was abrupt and held no hint of the longing in his heart to share games with Benjy. 'And besides,' he went on in an effort to prove himself superior, 'it's farther.'

The hint was, to Benjy, like water off a duck's back. He ignored it and started to climb the tamarind tree.

'Let's play Tarzan,' he invited, letting out the apeman's blood curdling yell.

Paul did not bother to answer. He sat brooding on his brother, and his hate flooded through his body and the blood pounded in his ears.

23

'Let's go over to Mac,' he suggested, undeterred and with his sunniest smile in spite of Paul's refusals; and Paul, because in the end Benjy always made him do what he wanted, subjected his will and walked along with Benjy.

Mac was the old shoemaker in the village and his shop was the meeting place of the boys during the holidays. Today the shop was empty, except for Mac, who was sitting on his little bench at the door stitching a shoe. The twins strolled into the tumbledown shop.

'Hello, Mac,' said Benjy, and went through the back door to the guava tree in the yard.

'Hello, Mac,' said Paul, and took a seat on the floor behind the shoemaker's back.

'Hello, boys,' said Mac, and went on with his stitching.

Paul picked up one of Mac's awls and began making holes in an old piece of leather he found on the floor. Benjy, out in the yard, was tearing off the bark of the guava tree with his teeth and pretending he was a wild animal.

A few minutes passed. Then Benjy shouted, 'Come and play, Paul' But Paul did not answer, he only sat idly punching holes in the piece of leather with the sharp awl. Benjy strolled back into the shop. Paul felt him enter but he didn't look up, he just went on pushing the awl through the leather and pulling it out again. Benjy walked across to him and touched him on the shoulder.

'Oh, come and play,' he pleaded.

At the touch of his brother's hand, Paul's blood surged within him and all the pent-up hate and fear and envy, all the accumulated jealousy and worship of the years flooded through him. His blood was hot inside him and he was blind with anger. He dropped the piece of leather from his hand and with one violent push, hurled Benjy into the corner. He ran across the room and stood over him, the awl poised in his right hand for a swift murderous blow.

Then he saw the look of incomprehension on his brother's face, the look of why, what have I done, the

24

look of puzzlement and surprise, and he saw the wide-eyed look of horror and fear in Benjy's eyes.

The awl dropped from Paul's hand and he turned away.

Mac had not even looked up, so sure was he that the boys were playing, so swiftly had the action moved. Paul passed Mac at his little bench and walked silently home, trembling and confused and frightened by the violence of his action; but purged of hate, and happy in the discovery that his brother also knew fear.

Theresa

When the pouis flowered on the hillsides, and the hills themselves were brown and bare and scorched, he remembered her. The sun-shadows chased themselves across the hills, darkening and lightening the valleys and the fields, making little bowls of shade in the scalloped hillslopes, and then he remembered her. Towards April's end, the land was sunbaked and windblown, and little explosions of dust occurred behind every footstep and the pouis poured yellow on the hills, and yet the rains did not come. It was then, most of all, that he remembered her, for it was at the time of the pouis' flowering that he lost her.

She was a lovely girl, brown as spice, and there was never a time he could remember when he did not love her. He had known her when they were very small together at the elementary school. She was a plump little girl with a pair of red ribbons in her plaits and, herself a boy, she laughed and played with the boys. The sound of her laughter was like a song on the air, but she had no time for him and she did not know how much he loved her or even that he loved her. They had grown together and she had become very beautiful, smiling from the corners of her eyes, but even at fifteen she did not know that he loved her. At fifteen, her hair gleamed in the sun and her spice-brown skin was a soft as velvet and she was beautiful as a young animal. He was very sad because he loved her and she did not know, and all the poetry he read was coloured with pictures of her, gay, laughing pictures with the sun burnishing her hair and the soft shadows under her eyes where her eyelids rested. But he had no words to tell her how much he loved her, for she was very beautiful

26

and he was very shy; and he was very sad, because she did now know that he loved her.

He sat in the Gardens one Sunday morning, and thought how beautiful life would be for him if he could hold her hand and run down the hill with her hand in his, and hear the wind whistling in the trees and the sound of her laughter on the air. He would be very happy and there would be nothing he would not be able to do if he could be close to the sweet song of her laughter, and there would be nothing he would want if he could hold her hand.

She came running up the hill. She held a branch of the flowering hydrangea in her hand, and it was lilac against her white shorts. Her bare brown legs were the colour of spice and she ran strongly up the hill on her toes. He buried his head in the book and pretended that he did not see her. He did not look up until he heard her voice.

'Hello,' she said. She was smiling and she seemed far away from him, remote and out of reach.

'Hello,' he said, his heart thundering.

The pouis flowered and the rains came, and in the flowering of the pouis and the seasons of rain, she grew and womanhood clothed her and his love for her was without end. In the time of the pouis' flowering, she told him that she was going to marry another man because she was going to have a baby. And for the last time, they went to the hill and watched the sun shadows chasing themselves across the scalloped hillsides.

'Everything is sad,' he said. And for the last time she said the poem for him. As at the first time, the tears ran down her cheeks that were the colour of spice, but now it was a woman's body that heaved with sobs. Her voice went on and a sweetness came out of her mouth, a sweetness and a sadness, and the years since the first time were as yesterday, for her eyes were bright with tears and the sun shone on her hair and her voice rose and fell like the swell of the sea. And at the end, her breast heaved and he held her hand and kissed her for the last time; for he loved her and she was very beautiful with the tears in her eyes, and his love for her was without end.

Her death soon after her marriage left him empty; but she was always with him at the time of the flowering of the pouis in the quickly passing years, and the sadness in her voice he never forgot; for his love for her was without end.

In February after the cane is cut and the fields are low again on the horizons, the earth is dry and loose and does not grip the weed roots too firmly. The dry cane trash lies lightly on the ground, and shelters the black earth from the blistering sun, and helps to stifle the undergrowth so that, having neither sun nor air, the weeds are weak and do not fight against the hoe.

A man working in his own fields and at his own will finds it easy to drag away the dry trash from the face of the land and dig out the weeds below, for the dry black earth will yield to him and under his feet, he will feel the earth in warm crystals; and joy and pride in his own land will make him stronger and happier, for it will seem to him that a strength comes from the earth itself through his feet and courses through the veins and streams of his body, strengthening his arms and weaving patterns of song in his heart and his soul. And above his head, the skies are blue beyond all description and such clouds as there are hold no threat of rain or storm. Around him, there is a skipping and a frolicking in the wind, and the smell of the dry can trash comes on the wind like the bouquet of a rich wine and a man working in his fields can work for a long day in the sun; and even if he does not pause to eat, he will not be tired in the evening, for the work itself will be nourishment and energy for him.

The pouis flowered and the seasons changed; the hills changed their colours from green to brown and back to green again; and the storms came and the lightning flashed over the Gulf, and the years passed. He was happy in his way, in the quiet way of a man who has had sorrow in his heart and knows that whatever comes, he can be neither happy nor unhappy again, but will always have a quiet soberness in him that will not be surprised. He watched the weather change from day to day and from season to season, and there was nothing that he wanted. Only sometimes when the hills were covered with the yellow pouis, he leaned on his hoe and remembered and was a little sad. But he worked in the fields, and the land was his love, and his love for the land was deep and everlasting.

The girl was tall and straight and lithe and her skin was brown, the colour of spice. She walked with a swing of her hips, and he leaned against his hoe and watched her walking with animal grace along the road. He watched her for many days walking along the road by his field, and he felt very old, older than his forty years, for she was young and full of life and very much like the one he had known before.

In the country, people are not strangers for a long time and the time came when they sat on the edge of the wall and looked out to sea where the lights of the ships and on the islands punctured the dark. It was very hot and the sweat poured down his back and stuck his shirt to his skin. Any time now, any hour now, the promised rains would come. Far away, over the Gulf, the clouds massed and a giant thunderhead reared itself in the darkening sky. Its outlines were hard contours in the dying sunlight, but its underbelly was grey and held promise of rain. The evening was brittle and he had a feeling that he could hold time and break it in his hands. Far away over the mainland, the lightning flashed off and on. The wind came off the sea, and although it was hot it carried a threat of coldness behind it. The evening had a certain quality of magic and the wind swayed her dress slightly and she seemed a dream child born of the evening and a wild, unreal fancy.

'It is very hot,' he said, quietly, so as not to break the spell he could feel around him.

'It is very hot,' she said, 'but any time now, the rain will come; the pouis are flowering on the hills.' Her voice was thin, a dream voice that was the voice of all the fairies of all the years.

The first showerdrops fell, few and far between, as large as blackbirds' eggs. Tomorrow it would be cool, and the rain would knock the blossoms of the trees and then the hills would be all shades of green.

'You are very quiet,' she said.

'There is not much to talk about,' he said.

'It is very strange, but I feel I have known you for a long time,' she said.

He started when she spoke. The sound of her voice was like a song half-remembered, trembling on the brink of memory, half-forgotten.

Off and on the lightning flashed in the darkling evening far away over the Gulf, and the thunderhead loomed in the sky. One by one the stars went out, and the showerdrops were as large as birds' eggs.

'Tell me about her,' she said. It was not strange to hear her ask. The words seemed inevitable, predestined.

He told her about Theresa, his Theresa, how beautiful she was with her spice brown skin and her gleaming hair and her voice sweet as music. He told her about his dreams and how he and Theresa held hands and ran down the hill, and the wind whistled about his ears and sound of her laughter was like a song on the air. And he was young again, young and very sad with the sweetness of his love. And looking at the girl who now sat beside him, he remembered how Theresa's skin was as soft as velvet and he told her that too, how one Sunday morning they had discovered the miracle of the poem, and how her voice rose and fell with the rise and fall of the lines, and at the end how her eyes were full of tears and he had held her hand and kissed her for the first time.

'She was very beautiful and we were very young,' he said.

The girl wiped the tears from her eyes in the dark and they held a silence together.

'It is very strange,' she said. The sound of her voice darted from him and he could not catch it.

He could feel her very close to him and he put his arm around her. Her body was slim and firm like a young animal's and she was very warm beside him.

'It seemed strange to me then, too,' he said, 'but it should not be strange; a lot of children must have read that poem. We were very young, you know.'

'I know the poem too,' she said.

'Do you?' he asked, a little anxiously.

Softly, she started the poem, and her voice was a whisper on the night, a ghost voice from far away.

'It is very strange,' she said.

Long-ago pictures floated before him. She lay her head on his shoulder and he could feel her young body very warm beside him.

'My name is Theresa,' she said.

The showerdrops fell as large as blackbirds' eggs and the lightning flashed over the Gulf. A star, caught in the thundercloud's edge, tripped and fell.

Galvan and Calliana

I

Galvan stared through the window; god though he was, he was unhappy. He was bored, more bored than any mortal can conceive. The fact that he was a god did not help him. In fact, it made things worse for him because, being immortal he had all the time in the world at his disposal and there is nothing (as all mortals know) that makes for more boredom than having more time than one can spend (some mortals say the same about money, but they are in the minority and their views cannot be considered representative). The millions and billions of centuries past and to come which Galvan had on his hands were a great burden to him, and what made the prospect even bleaker was the fact that, being a god, he did not share the gift of that hope which springs eternal. This is reserved for the exclusive use of mortals.

On the face of it, Galvan had little to complain about. He had had a brilliant career at school and university, where he had won all the prizes there were to be won and a few extra ones in addition. What was more was that it was only a few weeks since he had, by extraordinary order-in-council, been given a portfolio; he was now officially known as the God of Achievement.

No one had ever deserved special honour more than Galvan deserved his, for he had achieved much. Already he had solved the problem of where the fire went when it went out; he had calculated the exact weight of gold at the rainbow's edge. (He had done this by assuming that the specific gravity of gold of standard quality varied inversely with the square root of the water content of the atmosphere at any given time; certain mathematicians of the old school, however, were known to have viewed his results with suspicion.) He had measured the circumference of the mulberry bush (based on the brilliant theory that motion and commotion were really one and the same thing); he had solved the problem of making ends meet, had located the point of equilibrium of the standard budget, had, in a single paper, exploded the theories of the eleventh hour, the sixth sense and the fifth column. He had proved conclusively that the more was the merrier under all conditions (provided, of course, that values remained positive and finite) and he had, in his most recent paper, proved that dead heat and cold shoulder were equal for all negative values of temperature.

It was not only in the sciences that Galvan had made his mark. He had made a good many marks on canvas and his painting of 'Nature Abhorring a Vacuum' had evoked and was continuing to evoke much admiring comment. The Art Critic of the *Daily Oracle* had said ' . . . in his rhythm of line and absolute utterness of colour, Galvan has opened vistas of promise and set the universe free from the shackles of convention . . . 'His 'Youth Toeing the Line', shocking though it may have been to some of the senior folk, ' . . . eloquently voiced the cynicism of youth . . . ' and the intelligentsia paid reverent homage to the genius who had so unquestionably captured the spirit of the age.

At first, it was very pleasant for Galvan. He was invited to all the parties and he enjoyed pitting his masterful brain against the puny wiles of the designing mothers of young goddesses. He was invited to lecture to all the learned societies, and had received so many honorary degrees that some universities had to create special honours for his benefit. And he was especially glad for his mother's sake. She was delighted with his successes. She was in demand everywhere; for lectures, readings, committee work, and wherever she went, she was patronised and honoured because of her son. She had written countless articles for the evening newspapers on how to train a god child, and her *Galvan: Godling and Genius* was a compulsory handbook for use in schools and had sold over 20 million copies. Her prestige, firmly based on her son's brilliant genius, was unassailable.

The climax of Galvan's career had come a few weeks before when he was made God of Achievement. It was an unprecedented honour and Galvan was justifiably proud of his attainment. His chin jutted out a little more defiantly, his carriage was a trifle more erect and there was a suspicion of flourish to his signature.

But soon, very soon, it all began to pall and Galvan found himself not only bored but lonely. There was nothing for him to do and he had all the time in the world to do it. He had no one to talk to, for his intelligence had so far outstripped the rest of the community that they evaded him; and hostesses, who up to a month ago were begging him to come to their parties, had now given up inviting him because, they said, he merely made people uncomfortable. His friends began to dodge him in the street and even his mother had begun to fidget in his presence. He had solved all the problems, had achieved the ultimate honour, but his own personal problem of loneliness remained unsolved. To make things worse, he had made some enemies on his way to success. For instance, he had disproved the theory that an apple a day keeps the doctor away, and the medical profession was up in arms against him. (For a long time, they had encouraged this myth so as to further their own ends: now they had visions of a complete collapse of their power.) He had proved that a stitch in time saves not nine but ten point six three five (this had alienated the tailors and dressmakers) and his law of gravity – gravity is a force to be reckoned with – had so shocked the scientific world that a few universities (the minor ones) had withdrawn their honorary degrees.

And so, with the burden of time on his hands, Galvan stared idly through the window. He stared so long that his eyelids grew heavy. The burden of time fell of his hands and before he could say Jack Robinson (whom he saw passing in the street below) he had fallen asleep. As he slept he dreamt.

II

Galvan dreamt. It was a very bright and very warm day, and he was walking down a strange street which struck him as curiously empty, until he remembered that it was Thursday half holiday. Out of nowhere, it seemed, a woman appeared who bore a striking resemblance to Umbrage, the Ugly Goddess whom he knew but had not seen for a long time. Yet somehow, she did not seem very ugly now. She had the same ridiculous pearls for teeth and cockle shells for ears, but the combination of golden hair, ruby lips and peaches-and-cream complexion was less like a carnival mask than it used to be. In this strange street and under the bright light, Umbrage appeared almost passable. She must have seen him, for the moment he caught sight of her, she turned around and started to walk away from him. Spurred on by some compulsion he did not bother to analyse, he quickened his step and in a short time he was taking Umbrage by the hand and leading her through an open doorway which appeared on his right.

Now, Umbrage was brought up on the knowledge that gods do not like the ugly, and she was more than surprised that Galvan had bothered to pay any attention to her. So she was understandably curt with him when, after sitting at one of the tables in the room they had entered, he asked her what she was going to have.

'Lemonade,' she said.

Galvan raised his eyebrows, for Umbrage, it was well known, could carry stronger stuff than lemonade. But he said nothing. An old man with a shock of white hair came out of an inner room and began to wipe down the tables. He paid no attention to them, although they were the only people in the room, and Galvan raised his voice.

'A double rum,' he shouted, ' and a glass of lemonade for the lady.'

The old man looked up and stared for a moment at Umbrage. Immediately his hair turned jet black. Umbrage smiled.

'The shock was too much for him,' she said, simpering and powdering her nose.

When the drinks were brought (and paid for), Galvan turned to the goddess.

'I am not at all happy,' he said.

'What's your trouble? Umbrage asked, 'Money or women?'

'I am lonely and unhappy and bored,' Galvan said.

'You unhappy, the God of Achievement unhappy!' Umbrage laughed.

'That doesn't strike me as amusing,' Galvan said, a trifle haughtily. He took a sip from his glass, coughed and shook his head.

'And what makes you think I can help?' Umbrage asked.

'Well, you were the first person I met; and anyway, you are a woman of the world, no offence meant,' he said.

'Blood is thicker than lemonade,' the goddess said, taking a sip and smiling. 'Maybe I can help. I have been watching you for a long time now, young man, and . . .'

'I am a god, I must remind you,' Galvan interrupted, jumping up and standing on his dignity.

'I beg your pardon,' Umbrage apologised. 'I have been watching you for a long time now, young god, and I have come to the conclusion that what you need is a woman, a mortal woman.'

At this suggestion, Galvan experienced a feeling of revulsion; and jumped up and stood so heavily on his dignity that there was a sound as of breaking glass; and he woke to find himself standing over his desk. On the floor at his feet, his dignity lay shattered in tiny splintered pieces next to the burden of years which had fallen as he went to sleep. He picked up the bundle of time, but it was obvious that he would never be able to put his dignity back together again; so he left it as it was.

III

For many days after his dream, Galvan moped and drooped miserably around Elysium. Nothing satisfied him; he grew listless and bad tempered, and his appetite slackened. He spent less and less time in his office and little bits of gossip appeared in the popular newspapers. The community began to worry about him and a certain section called for his resignation, for it did not seem as if he was fulfilling his promise or the trust they had put in him. There was talk in responsible quarters of a reallocation of portfolios.

Galvan himself was entirely unconcerned about the gossip and the stories which were going the rounds of the clubs and bars. He spent his days searching for Umbrage and for the street where he met her. He travelled from one end of Elysium to the other asking for a shop with an attendant with a shock of white hair or a shock of jet black hair, but he merely confused people and had no success. Nobody could help him, not even Rene, the eldest Gade boy, whose help he solicited to go around the downtown spots at night after midnight. He grew more and more wretched until his father, who was worrying about him, suggested that he should go to the psychiatrist. But even this was useless, for the psychiatrist refused to attend to him. Galvan, it seemed, had offended him some time before by some remarks in his paper *A Short Note on the Relation of the Community to the Bogey Man*.

At last, Galvan decided to tell his parents about his dream. It took a great deal of courage for him to make this decision, but as he had lost his dignity, he found it easier than he would have under normal conditions.

'So you want to go to Earth to find this mortal woman?' his father said, when he had finished his story.

'Yes, Father,' Galvan replied. Secretly, his father was glad that the boy was going to see the world and wished he himself could accompany him, but he had to hem and haw to show that he was considering seriously.

'I am not sure it will be easy to arrange,' he said.

'Oh, I'll get a diplomatic passport easily enough,' Galvan said.

'I suppose so.' The old man hemmed and hawed. 'But there may be trouble about your re-entry when you want to come back. You can never tell what revolutionary ideas you might pick up over there. Travel is all right in a way, but it's a great danger, you must agree.'

'But surely I can be trusted?' Galvan said. But there was no dignity behind his words, and his father merely smiled and patted his son's head.

'Never mind, my son,' he said, 'I'll see what can be done. Meanwhile, you should get as much rest as you can.'

In the end, a visa was procured and Galvan kissed his parents goodbye at the airport and prepared to leave the only home he had ever known.

'Be careful, son,' his mother said, with tears in her eyes. 'Don't forget to get in touch with the Embassy at the slightest sign of trouble.'

The journey did not last as long as he thought it would and he arrived at his destination feeling quite fresh. There was a big crowd at the airport, and he thought at first that they must have come to meet him until he remembered that no one knew that he was coming. Then his eye caught Umbrage. She was looking very smart in her high-heeled shoes and her hair perched on the top of her head. She waved to him and he felt happier than he had done for a long time. He had not the slightest trouble with customs after he showed his diplomatic passport, but it was some time before he could escape the newspaper man who kept calling him Mr Galvan and asking him what his impressions of the country were and what was the purpose of his visit. To this latter question Galvan replied gruffly, 'Woman!' and the newspaper man's face assumed a shocked expression.

'He'll tell all his friends about that,' Umbrage said.

It was clear to Galvan that Umbrage knew nothing about his dream and he wondered why he should have thought that she would.

'Is it true?' Umbrage asked. 'I mean, what you told the newspaper man?'

'Yes, I'm afraid it is.'

'What on earth is there to be afraid of?' Umbrage asked.

'I had forgotten for the moment that I was on Earth,' Galvan said. And he proceeded to tell her the story of his dream.

Umbrage laughed uproariously at the point where she ordered lemonade, but when Galvan had finished, she grew serious.

'I'll have to see what can be done,' she said. And with that, she powdered her nose and walked away. And that was the last that Galvan saw of Umbrage.

IV

The country was beautiful to him. There was a quality in the light that made everything seem nearer to him than he was to it, and accustomed as he was to the dull twilight of the gods, he found the new sharpness in the light and the new brightness of the colours unexpectedly refreshing. It seemed to him that a new lustre had been given to every leaf, to every shrub and flower. From his window, he could look out on the hills and they fascinated him. He never tired of watching them, for they were never the same. Blue with mist and mystery in the early morning, majestic in the bright sunlight, and dark masses, mere shapes against the skyline at night, with the trees on the ridges stretched out like a camel caravan crossing the desert in single file. The hills were always either before his eyes or his imagination, and without his knowledge, there stole upon him the realisation that whatever the future held in store for him lay in those high hills. He bought a map of the country and planned an outing to the hills. From the hotel boys, he learned that the early morning about two hours before dawn was the best time to set out. In the chill of 'foreday morning, Galvan started for the hills. His spirits were high and he felt like a young god again. His way lay beside a river and through a wood. The dry leaves were damp in the dew and his footsteps made no sound. As he walked, now and then he could hear the scurrying of wood life and the plop of falling fruit. Then the track began to rise and he started his ascent of the mountain. Sometimes, he came across a clearing and the first faint streaks of dawn would come through the treetops. He was completely happy. Suddenly, without warning, he came upon a little hut set in a clearing. There was no one astir and he stopped for a while wondering who would choose to live in such a remote spot. As he watched, an old man came out of the hut, looked up towards the east and then, seeing him, said, 'Good morning.'

'Good morning,' he said in reply, but he did not move on.

The old man went behind the hut, and when he came back, seemed surprised that Galvan was still there. 'Hiking?' he asked.

'Yes,' Galvan replied. 'And do you live here alone?' he asked.

'Yes,' the old man said, 'and no.' And with this reply, he disappeared inside the hut in a huff.

Galvan was still puzzling over what the old man could possibly have meant when a girl came out of the hut. She was slender like a young tree, and when she walked she swayed as a young tree sways in the wind. On her head she wore a kerchief of many colours; reds and yellows and browns and greens. Galvan had never seen such a madness of colours before, and he watched the girl, entranced. Her shoulders were bare and her dress, which was of the same pattern as her kerchief, clung to her lissom body as a glove clings to the hand. Her lips were slightly parted as if she were singing or expecting something. She stared at Galvan and without a word started up the hillside.

'She is very beautiful,' Galvan said aloud to himself, as he watched her swaying up the path like a sapling in the wind.

'You must be careful, she is a flirt.' Galvan turned to find the old man standing beside him and smiling mischievously. 'She is my child and I tell you she is a flirt,' the old man said.

'But she is the most beautiful creature I have ever seen,' Galvan said.

'She is my daughter, not a creature I would have you know,' the old man said. Upon which, he marched off behind the hut in another huff.

V

The girl was sitting under a mango tree when Galvan caught up with her at last.

'Hello,' she said, quite friendly. 'I was wondering when you would catch up.'

Her voice was like a song, Galvan thought, and he could listen to her forever.

'What is your name?' she asked.

Galvan had never seen a girl so beautiful before. He could not take his eyes off her naked shoulders, black as the blackbird's wing now that the sun was shining on them, and she tossed her head so delicately when she spoke, that he was enchanted with her.

'What is your name for the second time of asking?' she asked.

'Galvan,' he said.

'Let us face facts,' the girl said, tossing her head and ensnaring Galvan even more completely. 'Where are you going?'

'I was going over the hill to see the sea,' Galvan said.

'Alone?' the girl asked.

'Yes,' he said, 'I had meant to ask Umbrage to take me . . .'

The girl interrupted him with a laugh that tinkled on the air like music.

'That's the first I've heard of Umbrage taking anyone,' she said.

'You are a clever girl,' Galvan said.

'I can see you are a stranger,' the girl said, 'by the compliments you pay.' She jumped up suddenly and ran through the grass. Galvan followed her He could do nothing else.

'Why do you run from me?' he asked.

'You are a god, that's why,' the girl replied.

'And what's wrong with being a god?' Galvan asked. 'Besides, how do you know I am a god?'

'That's easy,' the girl said. 'You have no dignity. Gods never have dignity when they come over here. They think they are slumming when they pay us a visit so they leave their dignity at home. I hate gods.' But she said this so innocently that Galvan could not take offence.

'Oh, you mustn't say that,' he said, 'Already I have broken my dignity and now you want to break my heart. You see, I love you.'

'I have had many lovers already, so that's nothing new.'

'Then your father was right, you are a flirt.'

'That's because I am beautiful,' she said.

'Now take Umbrage, for example . . . ' he started.

'No, thank you,' the girl said. 'I don't want her, you can have her.'

She skipped through the grass like a young animal, and the curves of her naked shoulders were beautiful in the sun.

'You grow more beautiful every minute,' Galvan said. But the girl was hopping and skipping through the grass and there was nothing he could do but run behind her.

'You say you have had many lovers,' he said, out of breath when he had caught up with her. She threw herself down and curled up in the long grass like an animal before she answered.

'Yes, I did say so,' she said.

'And why do you change them?' Galvan asked.

'I don't,' she said. 'They change me.'

'I should never leave you,' he said.

'Then you would bore me,' she said, tying the knot in her kerchief tighter.

Galvan lay on the grass beside her.

'What is your name?' he asked her.

'Calliana,' she said, pointing her toe and studying the curve of her ankles.

'Calliana,' he repeated, 'That's a beautiful name, Calliana of the naked shoulders.'

'What are you god of?' Calliana asked, as if she had not heard Galvan's remarks.

'My portfolio was Achievement,' he said, 'but I am not sure about anything any more.'

'Nothing is sure on Earth,' she said.

He drew closer to her. Her shoulders were black in the sun like the blackbird's wing, and the curve of them was the most beautiful thing he had ever seen.

'You are so beautiful,' he said, 'that I feel a fever inside.'

'God of Achievement,' she said slowly, as if her thoughts were very busy. 'Why, then you must be in charge of the end of things, finality, conclusions, the very things I hate; you must be responsible for everything abrupt and sharp, in taste and colour and sound and shape, the sharpness of knives, of staccato music.'

'I don't understand you,' Galvan said, but he could not stop the flow of her talk.

'The edges of cliffs, the sharpness and suddenness of lightning, all these belong to your department,' she said; 'the shock of sudden news, all things stark and startling, the snap of a twig underfoot, the humming bird's dart, all things sudden, swift and irrevocable; all sharp angles, delta wing aircraft, all things decisive, the clear cut edge of a mind made up, shut doors, curt refusals, judges' decisions, juries' verdicts, the end of the road, the having arrived, the having gone . . .'

'How you run on,' he said, drawing closer to her and taking her hand in his.

'Exactly,' she said. 'It's my nature to run on. I am your opposite.'

'What do I care what you are?' he asked, kissing her naked shoulders and expecting no answer.

'I am not immortal like you,' she said,' at least, I am not *myself* immortal. But I am the spirit of immortality. For I am the spirit of all flowing things, time, rivers, old men's beards and maidens' curves. I am the spirit of the curves of mountains, the curve of flowers on the stem and the curve of a bird's flight in the air. I am your opposite.'

'I see, Galvan said, for he saw that he could not stop the flow of her talk.

Calliana pointed her tow as a dancer does sometimes. 'I am the spirit of the curve of the instep,' she said.

'And what a beautiful instep it is,' Galvan said.

She smiled at him faintly. 'The arch of the horse's neck, all things gliding, falling, curling are mine, whether upwards like the hillsides or downwards like the waterfall. The going, the continuity, the travelling, the never arriving; I am the spirit of what can never stop – the spirit of

Love. But you, you are the God of the End, my opposite, the God of Arrival.'

Galvan could find nothing to say, but Calliana's body was warm against his and there was no need to say anything. Together, they lay on the grass and the sun was warm on their faces.

'Have you ever looked forward to Christmas?' Calliana asked. 'Yearned for it, and then, when it came, have you not always been disappointed? That is what I mean. I am the looking forward, the yearning, the longing; but the achieving, I leave to you. So, you see why I have many lovers. I hate all ends, the end of the road, the end of the journey, the end of the page.'

'I know what you mean,' Galvan said, 'I have passed through that myself. The end of the road is an awful place. There is no further to go. That's why I am here.' And he told her the story of his adventure, recounting the list of his achievements, and of his boredom when there was nothing left for him to achieve. He told her of the dream and his shattered dignity.

Calliana listened quietly, and then at the end, she covered his face with kisses.

'I am the yearning, the longing,' she said very softly.

'You are very beautiful, Calliana,' he said, 'with your naked shoulders.'

Upon which, he took her in his arms and disappeared round the bend in the path.

EPILOGUE

There was a large crowd at the airport to meet Galvan on his return to Elysium. (This had not been as easy to arrange as he had expected. He had had to undergo a severe screening before they gave him his re-entry visa.) His mother kissed him and told him how well he looked. His father could see at a glance that he had got a new dignity, and hurried him away from the airport before the newspaper people got hold of him. In the secrecy of his room, his father whispered in his ear.

'I can see you had a good time,' he said, 'you have brought back a new dignity, but you must be careful, especially in what you say to the press. Whatever you do, don't tell them that you got it over there. You'd better paint as black a picture as you can or else . . . Things have changed a good deal in the last few months.'

'What can I tell them? They can see I have got back my dignity,' Galvan said.

'Find something to tell them, anything. You can tell them that you didn't have to use it over there, so it had a good rest.'

'But I'd lost mine before I left,' Galvan said.

'They'll have forgotten that by now,' his father said, 'the public memory is very short.'

The Living Image

In his mood of loneliness and despair and hunger, the first days of November came to him brilliant with the promise of better days. All of a sudden, as the skies cleared to blue and the wind whipped itself into a frolic, bearing on its wings the long past memory of Christmas and the long sought future of wonder and the hope that the days to come would bring something for him, he felt an indescribable and piercing sadness that was more than sadness, for it was, though it was bitter, as sweet as sugar. And its keenness was sufficient to bring the tears of regret and hope to his eyes, yet a keenness which let him know that there was a future, that he was not a fool to hope, that this grey monotony of days and nights which surrounded him was not all of what was in store for him; that the blunting, deadening opiate of the days and the empty night of Rachel and the dull house, and the hopeless regret of Cassie gone and Strachen gone and his father dead and Granny sick and dying and his mother set apart from him behind the long time barrier of grim uncompromising face and fierce possession of her house and him and Florianne and his own smouldering rebellion, that this too would pass away tomorrow and tomorrow. And November, spilling the red blood of its flowers over the fences, filled him with an almost reckless hope that the burden of his memories and his love would pass away and he would one day be free, free as air.

Yet, although he knew for himself that he had need to be free, to be left alone to work out own personal and private salvation, to suffer, if need be, alone, although he knew that he would never amount to anything so long as he was hounded down by the warped and stunted people and surrounded by their blank faces and the hollowness of their words, he knew too that he had, by some manner of means, to continue to search for that one face and that one word which, when at last seen and when at last spoken, would have the power to transform all his future days into a wonder and a joy. He knew, with a high exultation in the paradox, that he would be nothing, not even himself, if he were not alone, and he would equally be nothing if he were left finally alone and did not find the object of his search. And, seeing now in the warm brilliant November the return of the season when once upon a time he and his father had sat and talked together and shared whatever lay in their memories and in the storehouses of their hopes and desires, seeing the clouds whiter than reality float idly across the sky, and smelling on the wind the indefinable smell of Christmas and remembering the Christmas Eve pig squealing in the backyard and summoning up the long gone scents, scents of late cooking in the kitchen, cake and roast pork and grease and the heat and the steam and the tasting and the falling asleep surfeited with a taste of this and a lick of that, and the coming and the going; and above all, the shining spectacles of his father, eyes whimsical, rolling over his half-heavy Christmass Eve tongue, 'Adhesive oleaginous, O, call it not fat!' and remembering all, he knew that the bitterness lay not in the absence of the past joys but in the futile longing for their reappearance. Yet, with Papa gone and Cassie gone and Rachel, for all her first promise, discarded, and the knowledge that they would never return, he had to continue his lonely search for their images which existed for him and for him alone, and for the echoes of their voices and the words they had spoken amidst the incomprehensible babel which overwhelmed him. For, if he did not continue, if he let the ever resurgent hope ever be stifled, then he knew that all would be lost for ever and ever. In this mood of November regret and hope, he went to see Walter Graham.

Walter lived in the village. He was Cassie's friend, and Cassie, who had known no father, thought of him always as his father. George recalled the very first time he had spoken to Walter. It had been a long hot morning in August when he had run away from home to play cricket with the village boys. When the real game was over and the other boys had gone, he and Cassie, reluctant to separate from each other, had continued to bat and bowl in the shade of the tamarind tree in front of Walter's house. Neither he nor Cassie had had much energy left, but he knew what to expect when he went back home; and they continued to play the desultory bat and ball, so tired and hot and hungry that they agreed not to hit the ball beyond the limits of the tree shade. From where they played, they could see Walter's house, and through the open window the music stand in a corner of the verandah. Cassie drew his attention to the preparations Walter was making to practise, and he saw him tucking his handkerchief over his pyjama collar and under his chin, and then resining his bow. His nearly bald head shone as if it had been polished, and he went about his business of preparing to practise without a look outside the window, with a set purposefulness that George was afterwards always to associate with him. He had a distinguished figure and an erectness of bearing which made him stand out from other men, a poise which immediately demanded respect. Yet he was not stiff, but moved swiftly and smoothly on his feet in curves and sweeps with never an ungainly nor an ugly movement; he put his violin under his chin and left it there, and with both his hands he flexed the bow, and then stared for a while into the empty air. Then he began to play Liszt's Liebestraum.

'He's only warming up,' Cassie said. 'If he knew we were watching him he would never play.'

They hid themselves behind the tamarind tree, only

poking their heads out to watch the movement in the window. Across the open space, the notes floated on the air, light as gossamer, fragile as bubbles. It had seemed to him then, that even listening was too crude, that somehow the thought to find a way of merely letting the music fall upon them as it floated from the violin, that any effort of hearing was a coarse insult to the pure music. Up and down the bow moved, and the music fell in curves in the wind, hanging tremulous upon the air for a moment, threatening to become visible before it finally fell. And sometimes it did not fall, but was caught up again in a sweep and taken far away, thin and piercing and wailing, floating as a feather floats when it is caught in an eddying wind-whirl, away and away out of sight, but never, never, out of the mind which carries somewhere in its far dark recesses eternal images of whirling loveliness and sad slow departing.

What echoed in Walter's ears, he wondered, that made him extract from a slim brown box, shaped like a girl's naked body and a few strands of stretched horsehair, such intimation of a world never seen, but most certainly known? What sound sounded, he wondered, in the muteness of the silent days and nights that had such power to illuminate and enlarge the vistas of the imagination? The song of love sighed and fell and died, but the echoes circled, magically visible in and out of the green canopy of the tamarind's foliage.

'Let us go and talk to him,' he said to Cassie. 'Perhaps he will play for us.'

'You can try,' Cassie said, 'but I know he won't. He is very shy.'

Nevertheless, they went over and Cassie introduced him and they shook hands. Walter's hands were as soft as a baby's, and his smile was so welcoming that they could believe that they were people of importance.

'I knew your mother,' Walter said, 'long before you were born.'

'George was wondering,' Cassie said, 'whether you would let us hear you practise.'

'I wasn't really practising,' Walter said. 'Don't tell me you were listening in all the time!'

'Yes,' Cassie said, 'behind the tamarind tree.'

Walter laughed, but he put down the bow, and George knew that he had heard all that he was going to hear.

The friendship so casually begun grew with the passing time, until George and Cassie were like sons to Walter. For Walter was, of all people, the most polite and respectful George had ever met. He never laughed at them, however ridiculous their behaviour was, he never offered his advice, but he was never too busy to listen to what they had to tell him. He would bend his head and put his fingertips together in an apex, and listen as attentively as if they were grown up. He invested every action with courtliness and distinction. There was never anything haphazard or random or on the spur of the moment about anything he did. Everything – lighting a cigarette, wiping the top of his bald head, turning the page of his music sheet – was deliberate and planned and bore the mark of graciousness. He taught them bridge, told them about his early days, when he played the cinema music in the days of the silent films. Never a Sunday passed but he and Cassie found themselves in Walter's drawing room, drinking mauby and talking and talking.

But for all his friendliness and his kindness, there was something that kept Walter from them and from everybody. A look sometimes crept out of his eyes, a look of vain regret and of pain, a look that said that somewhere, some time, he had been hurt, and the memory was a sad and bitter one. When George began to go to dances, he thought that, when Walter played at the head of his band, looking down from the dais at the dancers sweating in their embraces, it seemed that he pitied all those lost souls who danced to his music. He had a way of making his face assume the blankest of expressions and his eyes would

51

stare over the heads of the dancers at the roof, seeing nothing. Only the regular gnashing of his teeth would show that he was listening to the music and counting out the bars of his rest. And when the time came, he would put the bow to the strings and swing away into the melody and fill the room once again with his own special kind of sweet tortured music, so that the dancers, not knowing what sort of magic the master had wrought with his violin, would feel as they danced that they were important and beloved. Under the spell of the music, each and every one who danced would feel that here and now, if anywhere and any time, was the distant promise fulfilled. For the music, led by the violin, would work its way stealthily into each corner and crevice of the choked up dark rooms of each heart, and summon into the light the memories long since given up for lost and presumed dead. And the old men would snuggle more closely against the women's bodies and the young men, shy and afraid and shocked by the music was doing, would hold their girls far from them and half wish that the torturing music of the violin would stop and release them from their burden of sweetness.

There was something, George knew, that kept Walter essentially remote and distant from people. But he did not know what it was. Now, in this temper of loneliness, desperate in search of something which would give point and meaning to the empty days and the hungry nights, searching among the crowd's faces for that one expression which would say to him, 'This is for you. I have been looking for you as you have been looking for me.'; searching among the crowd's word for that one word that would say to him, 'Here is the key which you seek; go and use it and open doors and walk down the endless corridors of experience; go, hurry bravely and fear nothing, for you have the key and no door shall be closed to you.'; he remembered Walter. And remembering, too, the dead gone past; how sweet it used to be when his father was alive, how then he feared nothing but knew that all things were possible; now searching and remembering, he went to visit Walter.

Walter was writing music when he pushed the front door open.

'Hello, George,' he said, 'this is a good one. I want to play it at the Club, Saturday night.'

He went across the room and looked over Walter's shoulder. He was writing the tenor saxophone part for Freddy Jemmott. His pen moved quickly over the paper, and it was wonderful to think that these blobs and strokes would in a few days become sounds, and boys and girls would move their feet and their bodies to the combinations of these sounds when Freddy played.

'This is Freddy's solo,' Walter said. 'You know how it is with Freddy.'

And he knew. Freddy was a fine instrumentalist, he knew all there was to know about a tenor saxophone and he could read quickly and accurately, but he had no style of his own. He was a born mimic, at the mercy of every new style of saxophone playing. He was like so many others in other walks of life, perfectly competent to carry out orders, to reproduce faithfully what they saw or heard, but devoid of the spark which makes for original work. There are those who hear no sounds in the silences of the nights, see no faces in the empty spaces, on the blank walls, but who, having seen a face or heard a sound, can instantly and infallibly repeat it. Such a one was Freddy. Time and again, Walter had left him to improvise his own solo and when the time came, Freddy would rise from his chair, his short body barely taller than the music stand, and blow into his saxophone. But out of the instrument would come not Freddy's music, but the exact reproduction of one of the American saxophonists. No one could tell beforehand what would come out, Tex Beneke or Coleman Hawkins. It could be anybody, but it would never be Freddy, because in fact there was no Freddy. So Walter had to write all Freddy's solos for him.

Now they were all of a piece, even though they were not his own; so that even if you did not see him when you heard the music, you would know that that was Freddy Jemmott playing one of Walter Graham's arrangements. All the lilting phrasing which was Walter's signature was there, all the sweet torturing melody came out of the instrument and all of Freddy's clean lipping and clear crisp notes. And then, after the tenor saxophone solo, the whole orchestra, three saxophones, three trumpets, string bass, piano and guitar and Walter himself would, at the word from Walter ('Right home, boys') crash into the final bars, and the music would jump bouncing against the roof and fall on the ears of the dancers in a driving pelting finish, and it would be impossible not to know that this was Walter Graham's music, his whole expression. Always it was the same, and yet it was never stale nor tiring, but eternally fresh and never before heard. And now, looking over Walter's shoulder, George thought that the gift of making music must be the most precious of all gifts, for literally out of nothing the musician created something which he and he alone could create, something which did not exist before, but summoned into existence by a magic of creation, would not, however long time lasted, be made again. And this gave and would give the maker of music an immense power and this power would breed a calm assurance and confidence. And this was the reason why, when all was said and done, he had come to see Walter. Because he was a maker of music.

'This is one of the Duke's latest,' Walter siad, 'a good tune, but I have to arrange it in my way.'

'And your way,' George said, 'will be the better way.' He spoke without flattery or any sense of paying a compliment, for in truth, Walter's way would be a better way for him.

Walter finished the score and put his initials in red at the bottom of the page.

'This will be a great tune,' he said, picking up the sheets

of music which lay scattered on the floor. It's a pity you can't hear it on Saturday night, first time out.'

'I'll hear it when the boys are familiar with it. It'll be better then. That's what Cassie used to say when people teased him about you. They were always telling him that you only write new tunes for the white people, and he always said that the old tunes were the sweetest.'

'Cassie,' Walter said. 'Cassie, I miss him. I may never see him again.' And he fell silent as the pictures came to him of the laughing, carefree, bawdy Cassie, the faithful lovable Cassie straining to learn to play the trumpet so that he could take his place as first trumpeter in the band.

'I miss him too,' George said.

'It is strange how one person can fill a life,' Walter said, 'and nothing else is important. And when that one person is taken away, then darkness.'

He got up suddenly and said, 'What about a drink?'

'Yes,' George said.

'Not so long ago,' Walter said, moving through the door to the shed, 'it would have been mauby: so time goes.'

He went through the door and in no time returned with a decanter and two glasses. He poured.

'Say when,' he said. He poured a drink for himself. George knew that he was not a drinker and had never developed any taste for liquor. And this accounted in a way for his air of aloofness. Always he was apart from the crowd: he could be surrounded at a dance by all the stages of alcoholic intoxication, yet he held himself soberly erect, bending and smiling graciously, but never a part of the high spirits and the back slapping noisy drunken revelry. Now that he consented to 'taste a little one', George could not help feeling gratified at the compliment the gesture implied.

'I saw Rachel at the Hallowe'en Dance last Friday night, but I didn't see you,' Walter said. 'She was looking well, as usual.'

'I couldn't bother to go,' he said.

'It was a good dance; all the boys and girls were there.'

'But not me,' George said.

'I was talking to Rachel during the intermission. She said that she hasn't been seeing much of you recently. What's wrong?'

And before George knew, he was telling him all that he knew was wrong.

'Everything is wrong,' he said. 'And now that Cassie has gone, there is no one. I thought at one time that Rachel would be the one. Since Papa died, I have been searching, searching for something, and whenever I think I have found it something happens and it goes away, or I find that it was really never there in the first place. Rachel is just like the rest of them. She loves me, she says, but she never leaves me alone: she is always around, crowding, wanting me to go to the pictures, to go to dances with her, wanting me to stop drinking, always anxious to do something for me, to make me so dependent on her that I shall be helpless without her. But I'll get away from her. I must, Walter, get away from them all; Rachel and Mama and all of them.'

He was almost pleading, as if Walter had the power to let him get away but was withholding his consent.

'What do you want to do?' Walter asked. 'I mean, what do you want above everything else? There is always something a man wants to do; everybody has his dream, what is yours?'

'I thought you knew.'

'Very well, you want to write: do you think you will learn to write and write well enough to make a living?'

'It doesn't matter whether I make a living or what sort of a living I make. That's not important. And that is what Rachel cannot see.'

'If that is how it is,' Walter said, 'then you will write well. You will be yourself and it will not matter whether anyone thinks you write well. It is like arranging music:

you must have your own personal individual way. It may be simple, crude and unpopular, but it will be yours and no one else's, and you can be identified by it. And in the end someone will like it for what it is, because it is you and yours and they will respect it.

'After I left school, my father sent me to your grand-father, old Josh Lane, to become a blacksmith. I had always wanted to play the fiddle, but my father wouldn't hear of it. He had never heard of anyone making a living by fiddling. It was all right on a bank holiday to make fun, but to do it for a living was unthinkable. So to the blacksmith's trade I went.

'You have no idea, George, how cruel your grandfather was. I have seen that big red man put your mother's hands in the vice and leave her standing for hours in the shop. I have seen him throw a piece of red hot iron at her and your uncle Grant – you don't know him – he couldn't take it and he ran away. Look at your mother's leg, I think it's the right one: you will see a scar she will carry to her grave. You know why she got that? Because she climbed the hog plum tree in your backyard after he'd told her not to. The man took a live coal from the forge and held it in the tongs against his own child's leg until she fainted. That was to teach her not to climb hog plum trees. How long d'you think I could take that? All the time, I had this music going round in my head and couldn't even get enough money to pay for lessons. And at last old Josh attacked me, I don't even remember why: he chased me round the shop, and when he couldn't catch me, picked up a piece of iron to brain me. I ran through the door and out into the road. He was such a pompous, puffed-up man that he couldn't be seen running in the street, and that was how I managed to get away. But I couldn't go home to my father, he would only have sent me back; so I went to my grandmother, and there I lived and learned the fiddle. I might have been better off as a blacksmith, I don't know, but that's not the point. There are only a few people who are lucky enough to be doing what they want. The thing is that you have always to keep before you this shining goal of your desire and never let it fade, whatever happens; never let it fade.'

He stopped for a moment, buried deep in his reminiscences.

'But it is not easy,' he continued. 'I know it isn't easy. You may have to hurt all those who have done you no harm and who love you, but you will not be able to help that. If what you want is important, then you will have to hurt all those who say they love you and yet would keep you from what you want.'

'But I have no wish to hurt anyone,' George interrupted.

'I know you haven't. That's what makes it hard. You must choose whether you will take the hurt or give it.'

And suddenly, Walter finished speaking and sat with his finger tips together, remembering.

He left Walter and walked through the village. The grey tired houses leaned on their groundsels, and each kitchen shack in the dusk was alight with the evening fires. Over the entire lane, there rose the scent of fish frying and he saw in one fleeting moment the whole pattern of the village life he had known so long; saw in his mind's eye the gutting and cleaning of the fish, white roes like wax worms put by for special frying, the boning, the elaborate ritual of seasoning and folding, the tail tucked into the empty head, the ringed onions and the coal fires. In every back yard, the picture would be the same. Flying fish was plentiful and there would be fish on every evening table. It seemed that in this moment all his days were suddenly concentrated into one moment, and in this fleeting moment of his vision, he saw too that this village pattern was his pattern, that this was what he knew, that for all his being born on the Terrace side of the Regent Road, for all the restrictions which had been placed on his coming and going, the village had somehow managed to permeate his life and this would be what he would remember, always, always. For this village and these villagers formed a microcosm of the whole, and what was true of them, of their tight little economies, of their hardness of hearts, their inhibitions and exhibitions, was true of the whole land. What they mistrusted, these villagers, any deviation from the rigorous schedule of work and sleep and play and rum and furtive hectic passions, every one mistrusted; and when in the loneliest days of his coming exile he would wish to remember this land, all he would have to do would be to remember this November evening rushing into dark with its massing western clouds red like the burning coals in the fish-frying coalpots of the village women; remember the smell of the frying fish, the dry odour of sunlight on the dusty road; remember the little boys playing bat and ball in the rutted lane, the stand pipe running wastefully, the coarse obscenities in this distillate of all his days, and the past would then live again.

But he knew too that, though he would be leaving forever, and never, never be seeing all this again and this stain of regret could not be erased, he knew that in his heart he would never want to return, he would never be able to return. He would perhaps return in the flesh, but his spirit had exhausted all the possibilities of this place. In this quick moment, he had glimpsed the eternal tragedy, that in the unfolding process of time, movement can neither be arrested nor reversed. And this he knew was the reason for the longing in the hearts of people, struggling always to go forward to meet what they did not know, but always in their hearts hoping to meet and to kiss again the dead forsaking faces and to hold the hands that they had lost long ago. For although they knew that the pattern could not be repeated, still, because there was only one life to each of them, they could not be absolutely sure that there would be no repetition, that they might not, by some special dispensation, be vouchsafed a second chance; and they pressed on in the throng and hoped and hoped until their time came to be lost in the wilderness of their barren hopes and the desolation of their dead dreams.

Sorry, Wrong Jungle

Joe Toussaint spent his first two months in England at a small college in the Midlands where the atmosphere was cosy and only superficially academic. There, from the very beginning, he was made to feel warmly at home: he sang calypsoes for the first time in his life (as a sort of ambassadorial gesture), he played a good deal of cricket which he enjoyed and generally he formed a better opinion of the English native than such specimens as he had encountered among the islands had led him to expect.

During his stay in the Midlands, he looked forward to his inevitable visit to London with a mixture of apprehension and fascination. Alf, his roommate, a cynical Cockney who claimed to have lost his illusions about everything – justice, the Labour Party, the inherent goodness of the common man, the equality of women – long ago in the East London slums of his childhood, kept telling him that London was nothing more than a jungle.

'Nothing more than a bleeding jungle,' he said, 'as much a jungle as any in your part of the world.' Alf still cherished a belief that any place outside of Britain was jungle and Joe thought it would be unkind to rob him of this last and really quite harmless illusion. In any case, Alf's cynicism and his too frequent protestations of anti-bourgeoisism seemed to Joe demonstrably spurious.

Reluctantly, with Alf and a very Irish young man named Sean O'Connor, Joe left the college one Saturday afternoon in early July and set out for London. A man driving an old Morris gave them a lift to a point just outside Stratford where, he said, there was a stream where the fish were fairly jumping. As they drove along, the man adjusted the conversation to Joe's presence and began to talk about Tanganyika where he had spent many years and where what he referred to as Joe's people were a fine bunch, only now in danger of being misled by unscrupulous politicians and agitators. Then Sean took over with a mixture of blarney and plain nonsense which kept them amused until they got out of the car. They walked a couple of miles into Stratford, where they watched the swans floating on the river and drank tea at a mobile canteen which reminded Joe of the roti stalls around the Savannah in Port-of-Spain. It was a warm and peaceful afternoon and Joe felt the rise of an almost animal sense of well-being. No one hurried in the streets and on the lawns, yet no one was without purpose. As they drank their tea and Sean skylarked with the two girls who were serving, the clear blue sky, the couples boating on the river, the mellow air induced a deep contentment that needed nothing at all, not even the prolongation of the experience.

A bus took them into Oxford, past summer fields and through villages and tiny towns as picturesque and as unreal as picture postcards. They reached Oxford after dark and left it early the next day, so that the only impression Joe had was of narrow streets and old buildings and the quiet deserted lanes of a Sunday morning, with the wind gently ruffling up the edges of the trees so that they showed the pale undersides of their leaves.

London, when he reached it, wore a pleasant and oddly familiar smile. They boarded a bus near King's Cross for Alf's flat. The conductor was a West Indian and gave Joe a wink of complicity as if the two of them shared a secret about London, as if they alone had penetrated into the realities of this jungle and, of all people, they knew. Joe began to feel at home although, he reflected, he did not know where he was going to stay for the next six weeks. Before they left the college, Alf had asked him to stay at the flat. 'There's only Jean and me and you can get a kip somewhere,' he had said. But Joe had only provisionally accepted. For one thing, he had not yet met Jean and he was determined to be cautious. Alf was all right, he knew, but his wife would probably have to be led very gently towards the idea of having him in the house.

Jean, as it turned out, was friendly and entirely without airs and insisted quietly and graciously that he should stay with them. She refused to take his 'Thank you very much, but I don't like to put you out,' for an answer, and he was forced into a compromise. He would spend his first week in London on his own and then come to stay at the flat.

Sean and himself spent much of that first night walking. They went past the Houses of Parliament, crossed Westminster Bridge and gazed at the Festival Hall. Then they walked along Waterloo Bridge from which a young couple were staring dejectedly into the water, then into Fleet Street and the Strand and Trafalgar Square. When they tired of sightseeing, they put up for the night at a hostel near the Abbey where Sean had some mysterious contact, and where an asthmatic and very pale youth wheezed and coughed all night to the detriment of any sleep.

On Monday morning, Joe said farewell to Sean who, he suspected, was glad to be rid of him, but who did not want to give the impression that he was. Joe was then alone; he did not know where he was going to sleep that night, but his anonymity among the multitudes emerging from the underground stations was like a blessing. He remembered how he used to complain about the lack of privacy at home, where there was always someone breathing down your neck: you could never be alone – whatever you did seemed to matter so much to everyone else that you were a virtual slave. He remembered how he used to envy the sailors off the warships in the harbour, walking around his town, strange and free and uninhibited. Now he was a stranger and incognito. No one was there to burden him with concern for his welfare, no one cared about him, he could come and go as he pleased: he did not even have to speak to anyone unless he wished.

One of the housekeepers at the college had given him the address of a place in Russell Square where she thought he might be able to get lodgings. He must have looked a trifle doubtful, because she had said, 'It's all right, Joe, there are a lot of Indonesians there.' He caught the underground and went to try his luck.

He found the place easily enough, a respectable looking house. He rang the bell and was greeted by a young girl who had a broom in her hand and no expression whatever on her face. She didn't know whether there was any room, she would go and find out. He was left standing in the hall. The place smelt of dusty carpets and old leather, damp and mice, and he made a quick journey back to childhood and saw Old Aunt Phelia who lived up the road from him in an old house which smelt just like this one. Aunt Phelia was a stern faced old spinster who wore shiny black satin dresses, buttoned boots and, like Queen Mary, black turban-hats, which she skewered to her head by means of a long and lethal hatpin. She always carried a brown bag in the musty recesses of which she kept, for the children of the village, acid drops and peppermints and, in their seasons, mangoes and sugar apples and sapodillas. As the memory of Aunt Phelia washed over him, the old time smell of the squashed and over-ripe fruit mingled with the smell of the damp and musty carpets until he could not tell for certain where or when he was, there or here, then or now. Through a door on his right, he saw into a small dining room where a smooth-faced East Indian was eating at an old fashioned circular table. Against the far wall stood an old sideboard laden with china animals, a sauce boat, two large meat platters with a design of bright blue flowers, an antique brass gong and a pair of blind cupids. He began to smile at the unexpected familiarity of it all, and at that moment, the man who was eating looked at him and smiled too. Then the girl returned: she

64

was sorry, but there wasn't any room. The man overheard her, jumped impulsively from his seat, wiped his mouth in his napkin and hurried over.

'Never mind,' he said, in a shrill Oxfordish accent,, 'they really have no room.'

'Thank you,' Joe said.

'My name is Joseph Ghopi,' the man said, offering his hand.

'My name is Joseph, too; Joseph Toussaint, from the West Indies.'

They laughed a little, nervously like children, over the coincidence of their names.

'Good show,' the Oxford Joseph said. 'I once saw Frank Worrell make a hundred at Bombay. He is a very great batsman.' And then as if in gratitude, he said, 'Wait for me, I'll take you to a place I know – we'll get you something.' And he ran off up the stairs at the end of the hall.

They tried about half a dozen places without success. Some of the landladies were brusque, some were indifferent and all were supercilious. Ghopi was disappointed, almost contrite, and apologised to Joe as if he were personally to blame for the lack of hospitality.

'Let's try this last one,' he said. But this last one turned out to be a failure. When no one answered the bell, Joe remembered that Alf had said that London was a jungle. Ghopi had an appointment and reluctantly said goodbye, but not before he had given Joe the address of a hotel in South Kensington and wished him luck.

He was lucky first time, and that evening saw him installed in what was really no more than a cubicle on the top floor of a hotel near a square. He locked the door of his room, put on his pyjamas and went to bed, wallowing in a pleasant loneliness.

The week passed quickly. Every morning, he caught a bus and went off for the day, came back in the evening, ate at a tiny Italian restaurant near the station and went to bed. He found it very pleasant to discover the places he wished to see without a guide and alone. He wandered around without plan and without hurry. On the Thursday morning, he remembered that Alf and Jean would be expecting him at the weekend, and he could not help feeling that he had found a most satisfactory way of life and that he had never lived in any other way. He wrote them a note to expect him on Saturday. In the five days, he had grown attached to his routine of wandering around London during the day and returning to his room to sleep. He had spoken to no one but bus conductors and waitresses and occasionally to a sharp-faced Cockney whose cheekiness and wit appealed to him. He never saw anyone he knew. Once, while walking along the Strand in a drizzle, he saw the back of a head which seemed familiar, but the face that went with it turned out to belong to someone he had never seen before. He was reluctant to give up his hermit life.

On Friday evening, he looked around the tiny room and felt unbearably sad. He went out and walked around the squares and gardens, looked at the big houses and thought idly about the lives going on inside them. Only a few people walked in the street. A young girl in a bright flowered dress made him think of home and how subdued these streets were, how this light was different and how stiffly these natives walked. His footsteps rang strangely on this foreign pavement. Suddenly, he was sick for home. The light of this summer evening was as bright as it knew how to be, but how different it was from the light he knew, how polite, how mannered, how sober, when set beside the flamboyance of a July evening in his town, when, before it died, the light flared and flamed against the walls and hedges. His heart grew sick for the disorder now so distant, for the haphazardry of his town, sick for its carelessness and its lack of purpose. The girl looked at him for a moment and he skimmed over the lines of her face, a face whose scripture of thin lips and delicately upturned nose held no message for him. She hurried on and he watched her trail her fingers idly along the railings of the square. When she reached the corner, a boy came around from the other side and collided with her. Then he put his arm around her waist and they went off, laughing at the joke.

He was suddenly conscious of an overpowering hunger for the sight of a loose-limbed walk, for the sight of drunken man in the street, for the sound of a loud-mouthed defiant obscenity, for the vision of an exuberant female bosom. This London was not, could never be, his jungle. Involuntarily, he pushed a door and found himself inside his first London pub.

He knew immediately he set his foot inside that he had been there before. A shabby, wrinkled character sat at a table in the corner near the dartboard. A group of four sat at another table near the door. They stopped their talking while they watched him; he could feel their gaze on his back as he went towards the counter. He ordered a shandy, and when the man behind the counter turned away to mix it, he heard without surprise the low murmur of conversation, which had been suspended when he entered, resume its current. He had, without doubt, been there before. The man behind the bar wore a tweed jacket and grey flannel trousers and an expression that he had encountered in a previous experience, he was sure. The room had nothing unexpected in it: the few tables, the slanting light from the door, the grey figures huddled together in solemn conversation, the dart game that was in progress; all formed a tableau which, miraculously, he had always known. Nothing was more familiar to him than the wizened, dirty old figure in the corner who kept winking and making monkey faces at him. He took his drink and sat in an empty chair near the bar to watch the dart game. In the act of moving and sitting, he recognised the repetition of an action he had somehow gone through before, and the illusion persisted until his eye caught the old man in the corner winking and waving his hand at him. He smiled at this gesture of friendliness. The old man interpreted his smile as an invitation and came over to where he was sitting.

'Hello, mate,' he said, in a Cockney accent.

'Hello,' Joe said.

'Drink up, let's have one together. Come one, you don't have to be afraid, this is London, not a bleeding jungle, you know.' He spoke chaffingly and was clearly in good spirits.

'It's all right,' Joe said, 'you have one with me.'

'Don't mind if I do,' the old man said; and then, as if it had just struck him that the conversation had been struck up in an unconventional way, he said, 'Filthy weather we're having for a bleeding summer, eh mate?'

It had rained early that morning and the old man now told Joe how he had been soaked to the skin. He worked in a bakery and had to be out in all weathers with the deliveries. He was not a Cockney by birth, he came from Newcastle. He told Joe all the details of his life. He was married but his wife had been in a mental home for years. They had had a son who was killed in a motor accident. But he himself was very happy and, as a matter of fact, he liked everybody. What he always said was, if you can't help a man, you shouldn't hurt him, that's what he always said. Take Fred over there in the corner, for instance, the one with the face like Boris Karloff, now that was a bastard for you. He was once kind to Fred, had lent him some money, and now Fred just refused to pay him back. 'Wait a minute,' he said, 'I'll just go over and ask him for the hundredth time.'

He put his empty glass on the counter and went over the Fred. Joe told the barman to fill it up.

In a few minutes, the old man returned. He whispered behind his hand that Fred said he would pay him tomorrow without fail. 'But he's been saying that for Christ knows how long now,' he said.

'You shouldn'ta done it,' he said, when his eyes caught his refilled glass. Then he started off again: he was an expert at darts, better than anyone in the pub; he had his own special darts, no guesswork with him, he didn't play with any kind of dart and he never let anyone play with his darts. You've got to take a game serious like if you want to be any good at it, that's what he always said. He was sorry he didn't have them on him at the moment, he'd like to show what he could do with a dart, but he would have them on Saturday night, tomorrow night.

'That's an idea,' he said, 'why not come along here tomorrow night about seven? I'll take you over to my place where they have a decent dart board and some good players and a telly. We'll have a good time, Saturday night's always a good night.'

Tomorrow night, Joe remembered, he would be with Alf and Jean. 'I'm sorry,' he began, but the old man cut in.

'I like your people, you know,' he said. 'A few years ago, I met one of your boys. He used to work in the bakery, trying to make some money to keep him while he was studying. A nice bloke, he was, we was always together, a very nice bloke he was. The other lads in the place used to tease me because I liked him. But he was a clever boy, he used to study hard, a real gentleman he was too, wanted to be a lawyer. The other lads used to take the mickey out of me – 'Oh, go on,' they used to say, 'he won't remember you when he's a lawyer, do you think he'll want to remember you? He's educated.' But he was real nice to me every Saturday night we went out; Joe , his name was. Well, he passed his exams and before you could say blimey, he was a blooming lawyer.. When he left the bakery, he promised to write me as soon as he got back to Jamaica. But the other boys never believed that he would write to me. 'Go on,' they said, 'write to you? For what? Why, you can't even read!' Well, Joe went back to Jamaica and for a long time I never heard a word from him. I said to myself, 'Maybe the boys are right after all, what would Joe want to write to me for?' And then, just when I had given up hope, I got a long letter from him: he said that he was settling down and so on, a real nice letter. When I showed the boys, they couldn't say a blooming word. Joe was a real nice boy. I like your people, they're good people.'

It would have been heartless, Joe thought, to refuse to meet the old man the next night, and he gave him his promise.

Alf and Jean had arranged to take him to see some friends of theirs on his first night with them, but when he told them the story, they agreed that he should go to meet the old man. In fact, they were delighted when he asked them to come along with him.

On Saturday night they took a tube, or rather a series of tubes, and found themselves entering the rendezvous on the dot of seven. The old man was not yet in evidence and they ordered drinks and sat at a corner table to wait. Alf and Jean had been intrigued by the story and were more anxious to meet the old man than Joe himself. Every time the door opened they would look from the new entrant to Joe for some sign as to whether this was the man. But the old man was not punctual. Five past seven and still he had not arrived.

'Perhaps he's forgotten,' Alf said.

Jean answered hotly, 'He couldn't have forgotten, how could he?'

They finished their drinks. It was now twenty past seven and there was still no old man. The bar had filled. Joe fidgeted uneasily. Perhaps the old man *had* forgotten, perhaps he did not mean *this* Saturday night, perhaps he had not understood that Joe had promised to meet him, perhaps he never meant . . . and then suddenly, the door opened and Jean shouted, 'Ah, here he is,' for she recognised him immediately from Joe's description.

And there indeed he was, wrinkled, shabby as ever; he walked slowly to the bar without looking to the right or left. Joe watched him, waiting for him to turn and wave a greeting. But the old man did not see him. He leaned against the counter and ordered a pint of bitter, his choice of the previous evening. Then he turned and cautiously, almost furtively, surveyed the room. Joe waited for their eyes to meet, but the old man's glance passed over them without pausing: he had never seen any of them before. Joe felt Jean looking at him, but he could not take his eyes off the rumpled, derelict figure at the counter.

'Perhaps he doesn't recognise you,' Alf said.

Jean said, 'You'd better go over to him. Perhaps he's waiting for you to come over to him.'

At that moment, the old man took his beer from the barman and turned his back, so that when Joe, having made his way across the room to the counter where he was standing, touched him on the shoulder, he had to turn round to face him. When he saw at close quarters the tired, grey face, the stubble of beard and the nervous wildness of the eyes, Joe was more than ever sure that he had made no mistake in the identity. But the old man betrayed no memory of him.

'Hello,' he said, 'what can I do for you?' The voice was friendly but distant. It had the same shrill cackle of the evening before but neither welcome nor recollection in it.

'Hello,' Joe said, 'don't you remember? We arranged to meet here at seven this evening, don't you remember yesterday evening? You told me about the bakery, your friend Fred who was sitting in the corner?'

'Sorry, mate,' he said, turning back to his beer, 'you've got the wrong man.'

All of which Past

I did not at first recognise the voice on the telephone. It greeted me in a manner that I thought was elaborately casual: it was deep and within the limits allowed by the two words, 'Hello, George,' well modulated, but it was entirely strange. Its owner, whoever he was, took it so for granted that I would recognise it that I did not have the heart to undeceive him. The only thing I could do was to try to keep the conversation going until eventually I should recognise some familiar feature of expression. It was inevitable that, sooner or later, given only enough time, something would be said, the name of a place or a person called, a feeling conveyed, a phrase dropped, that would betray the identity of the speaker. Meanwhile, I could venture nothing beyond the neutral platitudes for fear I betrayed that I had not in fact recognised the voice.

'Hello, man,' I said, 'it's good to hear your voice.' I managed somehow to give the statement an adequate enthusiasm, not too little, not too much. There was a sound at the other end of the line a sort of gratified murmur and when this had subsided, I asked,'Where are you calling from?' There was no harm in that, I thought. The voice said 'Just around the corner from your place,' but there was still no give-away word or phrase. There was a little silence during which I tried desperately to find something non-committal to say. It was very awkward. Then, inspired, I said, 'What will you be doing at lunch time?'

'I was thinking,' the voice said (here there was a little pause,almost as if the speaker were embarrassed), 'I was thinking that we might be able to get some drink.'

The 'some drink' was a clue. Reuben was the only person I knew who used 'some drink' in quite that way. Most of the people I knew would have said 'a drink'. But, as far as I knew Reuben was in England. Still in search of the ultimate conviction, I said 'That will be fine, I'm always in the market for a drink, as you know. Are you buying?' That, I thought, struck the correct note of familiarity and playfulness. If it were indeed Reuben, whom I had not seen for six years, the familiarity of that favourite overworked phrase of mine, 'in the market', would be the correct welcome. There was a little laugh and the voice said, 'Oh, yes, I have some cash, I have some cash.'

Then I was sure. Without a doubt, it was Reuben; for it was a peculiarity I had noticed long ago about him that, although he liked to fancy himself as outspoken, calling things, sometimes brutally, by their right names, he never called money 'money'. For him, it was always cash or spondulicks, argent, pieces of eight, ducats, dinero, brass, tin. It was never money. This strange reluctance to acknowledge money by its plain name had once, long ago, helped me to a deeper and truer insight into him, and it was by this idiosyncrasy that I recognised him after six years. I was glad that he did not realise that I had not recognised his voice immediately, for this would have been an affront to his self-esteem that he would have found hard to forgive. I began to remember the sort of person he was: strangely enough, although he was unnaturally sensitive to any personal slight although he would sometimes construe the simplest and most innocent remark as an insult against him, he was as gullible as a child. He had only to imagine that he was being praised and he swallowed every superlative. He would fall for the most blatant flattery, but he was so suspicious that he believed that everybody was saying things behind his back. He was the most suspicious person I have ever met, but he was also without doubt the most credulous. If he suspected for a moment that my recognition of his voice had not been instant, our first meeting after six years would be almost as violent as our last one had been. We arranged to meet for lunch at the Chinese restaurant where we had both been so fond of eating before he went away, and I put down the telephone.

I could hardly believe, in truth, I did not want to believe, now that I was sure that it was he, that Reuben had really called me on the phone. I had not known that he had returned, and when I recalled the circumstances under which we had last spoken to each other six years before, I felt ashamed that in all these years I had hardly spared him a thought. I had read his novel about two years before, but I had found it easy to put him completely out of my mind.

It was a measure, I thought, of his supreme self-conceit that he took it for granted that I would immediately recognise his voice over the telephone: he had himself affected the most matter-of-fact of tones as if it were the most natural thing in the world for him to call me up, as if there had been no interval of years, as if we had parted on the best of terms. It was this pose of casualness, this old presumption that he merely had to call and I would come running to him that irritated me most of all, for he was not one to inconvenience himself in any way for the sake of anyone.

But in deepest truth, I know I felt immensely flattered. It is better, I thought, to be remembered by one whom you do not trust, whom you may despise, than to be forgotten by one whom you love. Love for Reuben I had never had. Once, long ago, this might have been possible, for I had then a warm admiration for his courage and outspokenness, but as things turned out, the most I could summon up was a sort of grudging respect which turned eventually into the bitterest contempt. And yet, now I was pleased beyond measure because he had called me on the telephone. Even so, such is the human perversity that I still refused to give him credit for any generosity and kindness. I was willing to admit that I was pleased, but I knew him too well, I thought, to accept that it was to give me pleasure that he had telephoned me. I had known him for twenty-five years and in all that time I had never known him do anything for the simple purpose of giving pleasure: he was much too selfish for that. His own self was the centre of all his thinking and I felt justified in turning my back on any manifestation of kindness. It was too late now, I said. Still, perversely, I was warmed by his calling me, and I reflected that since he had gone away and Cassie had died I had talked to no one. I was a little afraid now, for I should not know how to begin.

We first met, Reuben and I, at private lessons around Mr Thompson's table. He was two or three years older than I and had already started at Brereton while I was only then being coached for one of the exhibitions. Mr Thompson was a frightening man with a harsh voice and what he delighted in referring to as a strong right arm. He taught history by the process of dictating a set of notes on various battles, personalities and acts of Parliament. These had to be memorised and recited on demand. If, for any reason, they could not be recited in exactly the same words in which they had been dictated, Mr Thompson's strong right arm tried its best to whet the memory. This may have been a good way to get small boys to pass examinations, but it was most certainly no way to teach history. But of course, at nine, I did not know this, and I thought that my failure to memorise the notes on Lord Nelson and Mr Ramsay MacDonald was a sign of my incurable stupidity. The presence of Mr Thompson standing behind my back with the leather strap was no help, and I used to wet my trousers in sheer terror. What compelled my first admiration of Reuben was that he did not appear to be afraid of Mr Thompson. It may have been that, as he was already at Brereton, he felt that his future was assured: it may have been that he had even then seen through to the sadism and neurosis that lay at the root of Mr Thompson's brutality; it seemed to me, whatever the reason was, that it was Mr Thompson who stood in awe of Reuben. For instance, one of the strictest of Mr Thompsons's rules of arithmetic was that you had to show all the 'working'. He would take no short cuts; the simplest calculation had to be demonstrated, the most commonplace of arguments expressed; yet Reuben was able to ignore this with impunity, and Mr Thompson accepted his conclusions unaccompanied by the steps of the argument. I used then to think this quite wonderful, and in my heart applauded Reuben's bravery.

Sometimes, after lessons, we played cricket in the road, and I used to watch Reuben playing with boys much bigger than himself with ease which I envied. He had no real style as a batsman – he kept his left elbow too close to his body and his feet were strangely immobile – but he had courage, and what he lacked in grace, he made up for in determination not to lose his wicket. This lack of grace was a basic deficiency in his character, and it was his knowledge of this, I think, that made him sour. He had a good memory and was really clever enough, but he passionately wished to be brilliant with ease. He hated to have to work hard to achieve anything and he couldn't bear, for instance, to see Cassie laughing his way through life, easy, assured. The thought that other people could achieve easily what he had to fight for made him bitter. At one time, it prevented him from trying at all.

Cassie was my friend – I had known him ever since I had known myself – clever, witty and shockingly bawdy. He was older than I was, about the same age as Reuben, but I was easy with him in a way in which I have been with no one else. He had a much better brain than I had, but he never treated me with any condescension. We never felt any constraint in each other's company and there was never any need for either of us to discuss a question to understand the other's point of view. It was a relationship born of our instincts: even now that he is dead and his laughing ugly face and his rough voice are gone, even now that there is a desolation in my days that no one understands, our relationship cannot be resolved into words.

I had meant, before I began to write this, to avoid any mention of Cassie's name, but it is impossible to do so. What is more, there is nothing that I can write, there is almost nothing that I can think that will have truth in it if it does not somehow include Cassie. It was through Cassie that Reuben came to pay any attention to me at all.

When I got at last to Brereton and had said a thankful goodbye to Mr Thompson, Cassie and Reuben were already in the Upper School. I went into the Upper Second and it struck me then how great a difference two years can make when one is eleven or twelve. For Cassie and Reuben were moving in a world which seemed to me incredibly remote. Cassie never played games, but Reuben was already in the school second eleven and showing every promise of being one of the best batsmen that Brereton had ever produced. They were both members of the Debating Society, the History Club and the Music Society, bodies which had no use for second form pups. Cassie was doing classics and Reuben was doing science, and their respective choices seemed to me to illustrate the difference between them. Indeed, I cannot even now think or read of the respective advantages of the two studies without thinking of the difference between Cassie and Reuben. Somehow, in my own mind I see classics as I see Cassie, something fine and graceful and charming; I think of wit and tenderness. The grossness and crudity which I associate with science has nothing to do with the subject itself: it has all to do with what I used to see in my mind when I saw Reuben.

It was a good deal more than I expected for Cassie to pay any attention to me in school, and certainly Reuben would have thought it considerably beneath his dignity to acknowledge the presence of a second form boy. Cassie, however, treated me exactly as if I were his own age and in his own form and every morning I sat with the fourth formers on the steps and chatted as if I belonged there by right. Reuben, from the beginning, was inclined to treat me with the cruel contempt of which young boys are such masters: he was sarcastic and showed off in a degree which I did not think my relative unimportance merited. He was then, I remember, reading Somerset Maugham, and his conversation, studiously ignoring me, was heavily larded with the cynicism and the sexual details which our innocence at that time thought so shocking and outrageous. I suspect that it was because I was not impressed and because too in the little group Cassie was undisputed leader and my friend that precipitated the first clash between us. Cassie, he could not harm, but I was small and insecure: he had to make his show-off on me.

Reuben was, to all appearances and compared with the rest of us, well off. At that time, I knew no details of his private life but I knew that he was an only child and that his parents gave him all that he wanted. One morning, he came into the school yard with his hands in his pockets jingling his coins. No one paid any attention to him and so he emptied his pockets and showed us a wealth of silver half crowns, shillings and sixpences. It was a vulgar gesture, but we were all impressed, until Cassie said, 'The love of money is the root of all evil.' There was a loud laugh which was more relief than of any appreciation of a joke. Reuben put the money back into his pocket and sat on the step. Cassie turned to him and said, 'I have just discovered the perfect nickname for you: I christen you 'Rhubarb'.'

To this day, I have no idea what Cassie meant and have never been able to see the connection between this plant and Reuben's gesture. But I knew that Reuben's name was Reuben Arbuthnot Roberts, and the name Rhubarb seemed to me then very clever. Everyone laughed hearily, none more than I. Reuben could not bear to be the butt of the joke and the sight of a second former laughing at him provoked his attack. He came over to where I was sitting and threw me on the ground. As I lay on my back, I put up my feet to ward him off by kicking out my legs, but with a rush he grabbed hold of my shoes and tore them off my feet. I thought myself lucky to escape a beating, for I knew that Cassie alone would have defended me and he left me to fight it out for myself. There was a covered well near the third eleven field not twenty yards from where we were sitting, and Reuben, dangling my shoes by the laces, walked over to it, raised one of the planks that covered it and dropped them in.

Looking back at it now, I realise that Reuben must have known that he had gone too far. This was my first term at Brereton, my shoes were new and they had not come easily. If I had gone to the Headmaster, he would have taken a serious view of the whole thing. But partly through shock, partly because I had to prove that I could take a joke, never mind how wanton or cruel, I did nothing. I spent the rest of the day in my socks and bore as best I could the jibes of my fellows. Strangely, I do not remember, at this remove from the actual happenings, what I told my parents or what they did to me I can only hazard a guess that my mother, as she would have called it, cut my tail. But I do remember that next day when I went to school Reuben came up to me and put out his hand. I shook it, then he put his hand in his pocket and said, 'I will pay you for your bloody shoes.' I don't know where Cassie came from but he arrived in time to hear these words. 'Money is not all,' he said. The blow he gave Reuben on the jaw took him completely by surprise and knocked him to the ground.

The difference between Cassie and Reuben may be illustrated by a way I had of thinking of them. I was always trying to reduce the difference in the two characters and personalities to a single factor: in a a way, this was wrong, for sometimes an inconsistency in one or the other would confound me, but I was not very wise or experienced and had not yet learnt to resolve all the conflicting variety that often exists in the same person. I used to think that the basic difference between these two could be expressed most simply by saying that, whilst Cassie never remembered anything, Reuben never forgot anything. And so I was sure that the incident, as far as as Cassie was concerned, was finished. But Reuben would never forget. I waited and watched closely to see what would happen. But nothing did happen. I looked, I waited, I mistook shadows for realities, but nothing happened. At one time, it seemed that I was the only one who remembered.

Then, four years afterwards, something did happen, though not what I expected. At this time, Cassie was head boy and Reuben was Secretary of Cricket. In another term, he would be Captain and we all of us knew (by this time I was in the school first eleven) that this honour was all that kept him at school. The previous year, he had been *proxime* in the scholarship, but this seemed to mean little to him compared with the honour of walking on to the field at the head of the school eleven. One Saturday afternoon in the middle of the season, we were playing one of the leading teams in the championship competition. It so happened that one of our bowlers had had some luck and we were left to make 80 or so in our second innings to win the match. Arthur Barnes and Charlie Codrington opened and in a short time they had 50 between them. We sat back and prepared to enjoy the glory of a win against the leaders in the competition. Reuben told Pat, our captain, to put his name down at number eleven as he wanted to go to the pictures. I was standing near and I heard Pat say to him, 'I should have thought you would want to be in at the kill.' But Reuben did not take the hint. He put on his blazer and went down the pavilion steps.

As luck would have it, our team collapsed and we lost that match by one run. It was a very sad school which read a notice on the board on Monday morning. 'On Saturday afternoon,' it read, 'the school lost their match against Quakers by a single run. The Secretary of Cricket did not bat, he had gone to the pictures. I hereby summon a meeting of the Cricket Committee today at half past one in the library to decide what action should be taken.' The notice was signed by Cassie.

By midday, it was known all over the school that Reuben had sent in his resignation as Secretary of Cricket. I reckoned that he could not accept that for the second time Cassie would be the instrument of his punishment. When the meeting was called at half past one in the library to decide what action should be taken. Cassie proposed my name as new Secretary, and Pat Graham, the Captain, seconded. There were no other nominations.

It is now twenty years since the events I have related and it is not easy to place the emphasis accurately on each detail, but I cannot suppress the feeling that the events which led to his resignation, the resignation itself and the fact that he was succeeded by me, Cassie's friend, contributed to the wreck that Reuben eventually became.

Reuben did not return to school after the end of the term. We heard that he was married soon after he left school, but I never saw him nor his wife and I never thought of enquiring. At this time, I was beset by personal problems which have no place in this chronicle, and I had little time or energy to spare for those of others.

In the September of 1940 Cassie volunteered for war service: he was accepted and I went down to the wharfside to see him go. A group of about 20 youngsters was setting out that evening in the grey dusk. I remember it clearly. Cassie's mother was crying and so was I. I could not bear to think that I would not be seeing Cassie again. He was brave, but I knew that he was moved beyond words. This was the last time that I was to see him and I feared that from then on I would be alone. The thought of this aloneness was enough to make me cry. As I stood next to Cassie and his mother, saying nothing (for what was there to say?), Reuben came up behind me. He was wearing a scarf and over his arm he had one of the enormous overcoats with which the volunteers had been issued. He put out his hand and I shook it. Somehow, although it was Cassie's impending departure that had moved me to tears, I held on to this other hand desperately. Cassie would have been shocked, I knew, if I had clutched his hand, and so I had to clutch another. This Reuben did not understand and I did not want him to see that his going, too, reminded me that all my high days lay behind me, and all that lay ahead seemed a weak grey desolation of spirit. Reuben put his arm around me and I smelt the rum on his breath; it was the sort of expansive gesture Cassie would never had made, but I was more than grateful for it. They boarded the launch and disappeared in the mist that lay on the water. Cassie waved to me as if I would be seeing him the next day, but that was the last I saw of him.

In the December of 1949, I was walking along Frederick Street when I heard someone call my name. When I looked around, I saw Reuben. I had not seen him for more than nine years and he was greatly changed. He had put on a great deal of weight and I noticed a puffiness in his face; his hair was already changing to grey. It was an unexpected pleasure to see him and I looked forward to hearing as much as I could about Cassie from him. We went up to a Chinese restaurant in Queen Street for a meal. Before the food came, Reuben drank furiously, as if he had to slake a thirst that was overpowering him. It was, as I say, nine years since that bleak September afternoon, Cassie had been killed and I was expecting to hear all about everything. But Reuben said not a word about England or the war. Even when I asked a direct question, he merely shrugged his shoulders and evaded it. There seemed a bitterness about his mouth that was not explained and I wondered in what way he had failed again. I murmured Cassie's name but all he said was, 'Cassie, Cassie.' I did not know what he had on his mind, I did not know what had happened in England, nor what part Cassie had played in his life. Had Cassie been again the instrument of some punishment? I did not know then and I do not know now, but I know that the mention of Cassie's name moved him. I changed the subject and asked after his wife whom I had never seen. He said that she was well, but he said it with an edge of bitterness that made me uneasy. There was something callous, almost degenerate, about him and I was afraid for him. I told him that the Old Breretonian Society was holding its annual dinner on the following Saturday night and that I was going. Would he like to come? I ought to have been more careful, remembering the circumstances under which he had left Brereton. But he smiled, 'Breretonian Society,' he said, 'what is that?' I did not pursue the question but gave him my telephone number and left him.

On the following Friday, he called me on the phone and told me that he would like to go to the dinner after all.

I met him the next night at the foot of the stairs and we went into the hotel lounge together. A waiter came and I ordered a drink. The other old boys began to arrive. Most of them neither Reuben nor I knew. They were either before our time or after. There seemed to be a whole generation missing. The old ones were dressed in their white ties and tails, products of an older, more formal age than ours: they bent courteously and sipped their drinks and their jokes seemed to us as old as Homer. The young wore lounge suits and flashy American ties and their jokes seemed as crude and as callow as themselves. With them we seemed to share nothing. When we began to chat, we discovered that of all the 30 or 40, we two alone, Reuben and I, represented that period shortly before 1939 when one age was changing and giving place to a more hectic one. We alone of them all knew of certain masters, of the destruction of the old pavilion and the building of the new: the old did not know of any change at all and the young did not know that things had not been always as they were. We were alone together and I suddenly felt that I could not bear it. I felt that I did not belong and that it would be a farce to sit down with people with whom there was so little to share. The common experience of Brereton counted for nothing, for we alone seemed to know that the world was vast and lonely. The old were comfortable, resigned and corpulent; the young were eager and animal and athletic, but we were caught between them, neither one thing nor the other. We had learnt that the world was various, but we had settled for no element of its variousness. Reuben said suddenly, 'We are out of place,' and I agreed with him. When the rest were going into dinner, the two of us crept down the stairs and went into one of the night clubs on Park Street.

And so began a period of drinking and late nights which lasted for more than three years. It seemed to me that Reuben drank to prove something; what it was, I don't know. Sometimes he was placid and easy, at other times querulous and pugnacious. He had got himself a job as an insurance salesman and, as far as I could gather, when he stirred he could sell fairly well, but he didn't stir very much. Every afternoon he would call me on the telephone and he would sound so lonely and desperate that I would arrange to meet him, and we would eat Chinese food and then go to a night club. We came to be very well known and when Reuben passed out – he did this almost every night – there was always someone to take him home. But although we spent so much time together, we knew very little of each other. He had no interest, he had never had, in anyone but himself, for he was the most egocentric of individuals. And as for men, I could not summon any curiosity about a man for whom I had really very little respect and who, I knew, cared next to nothing about me. When he got drunk sometimes, he would curse everyone in sight; he once told me that the trouble with me was that I had a fourth rate intelligence masquerading under a high brow. I did not argue with him and he took my silence to mean that I was humouring him. I came near to hitting him that night. Next afternoon, he rang me up and we ended up drinking as usual. But his boorishness tired me. I was more often than not having to keep him out of trouble. I had always known that he was ungenerous and unmannerly, but his complete lack of consideration for others appalled me. He would say the most unkind things about people to their faces and express surprise when they were hurt. In his cups, he affected an English accent and in it he laid down the law on all sorts of questions about which he was totally ignorant. Yet, for some reason, I was loath to leave him. I wanted him to realise that, though he insulted me frequently, I recognised the insults, for he was supercilious enough to believe that I did not understand the insults or was too weak to do anything about them. But he was so desperately poor in spirit, so lacking in any redeeming feature that it hurt my heart to leave him, as it were, to the dogs.

The issue was resolved sooner than I expected. We had gone to eat Chinese food as usual and when the waitress came to serve us, he put out his hand and attempted to fondle her. She avoided him as tactfully as she could, but he persisted. When, in the end she told him to behave himself, he shouted, 'And what the hell do you think you are? I can pay.' My mind went back immediately to that morning twenty years before in the Brereton quadrangle, and I was sickened. I called for a drink and managed to order the meal without mishap. He sat at his place, brooding and sullen, and he did not speak. After the meal, I tried to suggest that he should go home, but he refused. I promised that I would stay long enough to have a single drink with him and then I should leave him to himself.

The night club was almost empty. The woman at the cash register was asleep with her arms embracing the register. She looked up for a moment and said hello. Two men were standing at the juke box which was blaring so loudly that we could not hear ourselves speak. Reuben said to the woman at the cash register, 'Bitch-face, I wonder if I could buy some silence in this place.' The woman smiled sleepily as if she did not hear what he said. We sat at a table and ordered a drink. When it came and I had begun to sip it, a woman whom I had never seen before came up to the table. She did not look like one of the regulars, but I could not be sure. She went over to Reuben who had his head bent forward between his arms and resting on the table. I did not hear what she said to him,but I saw him put his hand in his pocket and take out a dollar bill which he threw at her. It fell in her lap but she did not take it in her hands. She moved from her chair and the money fell to the floor. She moved away and left it on the floor. I heard Reuben's voice, thick and rough with drink, say, 'Pick it up.' I pushed my chair away from the table and said, 'Don't be a fool, Rhubarb.' I had not meant to use the old nickname, but under the stress of the behaviour so much like what I knew had given him the name, it had slipped from me. This made him angry and he pushed the table so violently that he overturned it and spilled the drinks and broke the glasses. I could see the dollar bill lying on the floor. The woman stood nervously clutching her handkerchief. She attempted to move, but he grabbed her savagely by the wrist. 'I say, pick it up.' His voice was low and ugly. The juke box had stopped and the few people in the club waited anxiously to see what would happen. The woman bent but her pride got the better of her; she did not want to so humiliate herself in front of the crowd. Reuben twisted her arm, 'Pick up the —— dollar,' he said. The woman was terrified and she bent and picked the dollar off the floor. He smiled and said gruffly, 'Let's dance now.' They clutched each other and passed near to me. The woman was crying, but on Reuben's face there was such a look of triumph, such a leer as I had never seen on him before. I have never despised a human being as much as I despised Reuben that night. When he finished the dance, I went over to him. I could not stand the smile and I hit him in his face. He was drunk and fell to the floor in a heap. And there, lying on the floor, was the last I had seen of him. I heard soon after that he had gone back to England.

Two years ago, I read Reuben's first novel, *Bright and Early*. It was an unsatisfying book. It seemed to me to lack truth and insight. It was little more than a catalogue of superficialities and betrayed the lack of imagination which I had long suspected lay at the root of his selfishness and cruelty. He simply could not think of anything outside himself; or to put it another way, he included himself in everything he thought of. Still, the book had had a reasonable press and I had to admit that I might easily be wrong.

As for myself, the years that had passed had wrought their changes. My life had not been smooth, and now that the turbulence had gone from it, I had settled for the dullest routing of work and food and sleep. I did only the reading I could not avoid except for the faithful few I re-read every year: *Pickwick Papers, Wind in the Willows, Alice in Wonderland* and the first chapter of the Book of Kings. What ambition I ever had I had come to deny, and so I had lost a good deal of the tension and anxiety which had troubled me when I was younger. Life was very short, I thought, too short for a man to spend it in frustration: he had, as soon as he could, to resolve the inevitable conflict between his duty and his desire, and recognise that what was true and good for himself might very well be false and evil for someone else; but he had to recognise too that this was the only truth he could ever hope to know. For me, it was as simple as that.

And now that the first flush of pleasure at Reuben's call had evaporated, I realised that I did not, after all, wish to meet him. What was past was past. I bore him no ill will, I did not in fact think of him at all; but I did not wish to be disturbed, I did not wish to become involveed in any life that was not my own, nor in any events except of my own making. I argued with myself that the kindest thing I could do for Reuben would be to avoid him. He would be angry, he would interpret my not meeting him as a rejection of him, but it would be for the better, I thought. I did not care as much as I used to what people thought of me, and I had no particular reason to desire the goodwill of Reuben, of all people.

But habit is a hard taskmaster: I had promised and I had never been one to take promises lightly. My innate curiousity had only been quietened, it had not been quenched; and, after all, I went.

Reuben was sitting in the bar when I went up the stairs. Except for his hair, which now grew in a thick mat, on the surface he had changed very little.

'Greetings,' I said, in the old way, as if I had seen him only yesterday. 'I am glad to see you, I didn't know you were back.'

'Don't you read the newspapers?' he asked. 'There's been nothing else in them for a week. I've been to six cocktail parties already.' His manner was easy and mildly self-disparaging.

'I've given up reading newspapers,' I said 'I make do with the headlines, it saves time.'

'What have you got to do?'

'Nothing,' I said, 'and that takes all my time.' The conversation fell flat. It seemed that we had exhausted ourselves in this slight skirmish.

After a pause, I said, 'I read your novel.'

'What did you think of it?' he asked.

'Not much.' I had no wish to be kind.

He laughed. 'It was nothing at all,' he said, 'nothing at all. I'm ashamed of it, but people do not understand.'

I felt very wise, and said, 'They never have understood.'

He looked at me closely, and then said 'I was only half expecting you to turn up. When I didn't see you after a week, I thought you were avoiding me.'

'I didn't even know you were here.'

'Even after I rang you up, I didn't think you would come,' he said.

'I very nearly didn't,' I told him.

It was unexpectedly easy now to speak frankly and without bitterness and the air was cleared between us. There was no pretence.

'I have my second novel coming out in the autumn,' he said, and I smiled at the Englishness of the definition of the time of year. My smile hurt him, and he said, 'I'm sorry.' He went on to speak quickly.

'I would like to dedicate it to you and Cassie,' he said. 'Would you mind? I don't think that Cassie would.'

I had not expected this. All the years fell away in a moment, and Cassie and Reuben and I were revealed in all the nakedness of our youth. I could not speak. People came and went in the room, but all I could see were the pictures of Mr Thompson's round table, the Brereton quadrangle and cricket field and Cassie waving goodbye across the misty water. In my heart, I cried out for Cassie, for he alone of us would have known what to say and how to say it.

'I did not expect this, never; never this kindness from you,' I said.

'Why?' Reuben asked.

I could not answer. The years seemed full of misunderstanding. For why indeed did I not expect it? I could not bear to think of my own blindness, my own uncharity.

'Why,' he asked again, 'why did you not expect kindness from me?'

What could I say? Why does one man not expect kindness from another? Could I tell him that in all the years I had never known him do anyone a kindness? That would be now no answer. Could I say to him that he was not the sort of man to do a kindness? There was so much that I did not understand. 'I do not know,' I said, humiliated past the thinking of it.

He said nothing at all, but sat staring through the window at the people walking in the street below.

'London was never like this,' he said, irrelevantly but kindly.

I looked at his face, the same face I had hit and Cassie had hit: the sharpness was still there, but I could see no signs of the aggressiveness and cruelty I had known.

'It is very kind of you, Rhubarb,' I said, 'it will make me very happy to see my name in print. Thank you very much.' But the words had a poor quality and a shoddiness that I could not help.

We shook hands. 'Let's have the drink I promised to buy,' he said. I shook my head.

'Not now,' I said, 'another time.' He nodded his understanding and I left him in the bar. There was nothing more to say and I was ashamed.

Call it a Long Farewell

Henry did not recognise, as he sat alone at the breakfast table, that this was the end he had so devoutly wished for, for the three years he had been married. From long habit, he sat sideways in his chair and swallowed mouthfuls of cocoa and bread and butter and buried his head behind the paper just as he had always done, failing to remember that there was no offending presence across the table to haunt him. In any case, the empty place irritated him more than the presence itself used to, since it was now no longer possible to think of himself as a martyr and console himself with the thought. He was confused; he could not make up his mind whether he hated her now more than he had ever done before, or whether her absence made him love her again as he used to in the days that seemed long, long ago. Love and hate, it seemed to him, were so close together, the sides of a coin, perhaps, that he could not tell where one began and the other ended. Mabel had made him look a complete fool, and he would never be able to forget that; that much was certain, but now on this first morning after she had left, as he sat alone, hiding behind his paper from her absent presence, he realised that already he was missing her. Could it be that he loved her still? He chased the thought from him. Certainly not. He hated her, she was a fool, a great big ox of a fool. He was well rid of her and if she thought that he was going to beg her to come back to him, well, she was mistaken.

This newspaper-at-the-breakfast-table habit was one Henry had developed after the first few days of marriage, reasoning with his usual illogic that when you did not see your pursuers you were unseen by them. His own experience had given him a sort of sympathy with the ostrich who, after all, he told himself, must have a point of view.

It was of significance that in his own mind Henry had identified himself with the ostrich and the pursued. No amount of detailed analysis could provide any real reason for his conclusion, but Henry, true to his lifelong putting-the-cart-before-the-horse practice of twisting his argument to suit a pre-accepted conclusion, could not and would not reject it merely because the reasoning which led to it was suspect. Only the fierceness with which Henry maintained his convictions gave any validity to the conclusions themselves. As far as he was concerned, he was the ostrich, the pursued, the hunted, and there the matter rested.

Henry, hiding from any empty place across the table, was not really reading the newspaper. He hardly ever did under normal circumstances, and this morning the circumstances were the reverse of normal. Yesterday afternoon he had come in from work to find a letter on the centre table in the drawing room addressed to him in Mabel's big schoolgirlish writing. It was a short letter and could not have been more to the point.

Dear Henry, (it said,) *I cannot understand why I waited so long to see that our marriage was a failure from the start. Today was inevitable from the very afternoon we were married and our marriage was nothing more than a preparation for this final goodbye; call it, if you like, a long farewell! But things never happen before their time.*

Yours, Mabel

That was all she had left for him, a scrap of paper with some words on it, words with no hint among them of why she had left, where she had gone or what she planned to do; only a scrap of paper with some words on it, words which had the power, it seemed, to hurt him and make him want to weep. Somewhere, long before, he had read that words were implements just as swords and spears are implements, and they had the power to hurt and wound just as weapons had; yes, and they had the power to kill too. Now, he knew it was true and it took Mabel, stupid, ignorant Mabel whom he had despised, to teach him that. How aptly she had summed it up. He had never imagined that she had it in her to see their whole life together in such real perspective and to describe it with such skill, such comprehension. Indeed, their marriage *was* nothing more than a long farewell, that's exactly what it was. How wrong he had been about Mabel! The woman who could sum up three years of life together in such a telling phrase was not the fool he had imagined her to be. It surprised him that it was only now that she had left that he could find anything to admire in her. Life had treated him shabbily. Always he had been right and she had been wrong. What right had things to go turning around like this? How could he maintain his rôle as the ostrich, the pursued, now that she had run away from him? He made a desperate attempt to reassess the whole situation in the light of the latest developments, with the conclusion already accepted that he was the wronged party.

Starting at the very beginning, Henry's mind went back to a time when he was not the pursued. There was a time, he was willing to admit, when he had been the hunter. There was a time when he had pursued her right into her father's house and whispered endearing things to her, had hunted her with expensive presents and the promise of an abiding love, with flattery and attention. But going over the past and finding it incompatible with the present (unless he wanted to admit that he was wrong then), Henry was forced to the conclusion that perhaps in those days of courtship, even then he had not really been the hunter; perhaps he had only imagined that he was, while, in reality, the woman who used to sit across the breakfast table was herself the hunter. Perhaps she had subtly managed merely to make him think he was pursuing her. When this avenue of escape from the admission of his own weakness presented itself, he pounced on it with triumph and returned to his old conclusion, more convinced than ever of Mabel's evil genius and his own martyrdom.

There was neither order nor coherence in Henry's assessment of the whole situation. He had not really tried to put the events into any form to recognise and appreciate their significance. With him, it was merely a matter of finding a way to convince himself that what he believed was, in fact, the only thing to believe. His mind was a patchwork of hastily conceived notions, fleeting impressions and invalid conclusions, a hodge-podge of self-blame and self-righteousness, of conceit and contrition. In short, Henry was like the large majority of other men; innocent but ignorant, unselfish but uncharitable.

There was a time, Henry recalled, gazing over the top of his paper at the empty place, when for him the woman who used to sit there was the most beautiful woman in the world. He had studied her tall, queenly figure, her coal-black hair and the easy grace of her carriage. There was a time when every action of hers had something of fineness in it, a proud quality of assurance and poise which he had never encountered in any other woman. With an adeptness born of long practice, he had jumped to the conclusion that she must have sprung from a long line of royalty. Her ancestors, he decided, were over-six-foot giants who beat their drums and danced their fierce, beautiful dances and waved their long spears in the moonlight beside the rivers of Africa. She figured in his thoughts as the queen of them all, magnificent in her six-foot stature and dignity.

Henry was never sure exactly when his love ceased for the woman across the breakfast table; but he believed that it was on the evening of their wedding, when he turned round in his seat in the front row of the chapel at the first massive chord of the organ. He had been staring in front of him at a tiny shaft of sunlight that was coming through the western door and burnishing the brass candlesticks on the altar. He had been thinking of nothing in particular, not even of her; his mind was a complete blank as he sat there next to the bestman, staring at the sun shaft and the organist's nimble fingers. When he saw the organist give a sudden glance towards the door and heard the feet shuffling in the porch, he turned his head and saw the bridal party coming up the aisle. But he did not see his queen. All he saw was a ridiculous white-gowned figure standing next to an elderly man with a bald head and moving up the aisle slowly and massively like an ox. A sudden fear struck him that he had been tricked. This was not, could not possibly be, the woman he had so passionately worshipped. When the bride came alongside him, he looked at her and almost failed to recognise the over-powdered face, topped by such a ridiculous head piece, as belonging to the queen he had won for his bride. His responses to the parsons's droning questions were dazed and inaudible, anger with himself swelled up inside him, and his love was stillborn.

Having concluded from the wedding afternoon that Mabel was a dull-witted ox, Henry set about to find his reasons for this conclusion. He found this surprisingly easy: what he wanted to see, he saw. There was no poetry in her, he wailed to himself, no imagination, just a huge lump of brawn and bone. He found as many reasons to despise her now as he had found to adore her then: she was now silly and frivolous where she had formerly been sweet and simple; where she had been reserved, she was now inarticulate, and her magnificent physique was no longer a tribal heritage but the result of some form of arrested glandular development. Her voice, deep-throated and musical, was now over-masculine, her attentiveness a clumsy pretence.

There was no conversation between Mabel and himself, no real conversation, that is, no sharing of deep down secrets as between man and wife; two separate units of thought and emotion walked around the house and sat down to meals together, each in a separate world which was untrespassed by the other.

Much as he despised his wife and derided her animal-like simplicity, much as he denied her intelligence and a mind of her own, Henry was afraid of her. Her eyes, so clear and trusting, so without guile, still seemed to have the power to shrivel him up into something seen through the wrong end of a telescope. He felt an unwholesome insignificance and it made him boisterous and sarcastic. It was at this time that he developed the habit of hiding behind the morning paper. Every now and then he would raise he eyes above the level of the paper to see what the woman across the table was doing. Invariably, two brown eyes would be staring frankly back at him and he would have to bury his head hastily in confusion. The newspaper was a wall between himself and the other side of the table, nothing more.

'Henry,' she had said to him one day, 'please take me to the art show next week.' Her voice was trusting and childlike, too trusting and childlike for him not to suspect a subterfuge.

'Oh,' he said, trying to make it sound casual and hiding the irritation he felt, 'you wouldn't understand it. What's the point of going?' He was outraged by the monstrosity of her suggestion. It was so ridiculous that he wanted to laugh. What did she want to go to an art show for? A circus was more in her line. But what did she understand anyway? Did she understand anything at all? Yet, surely, she couldn't be as dumb as she looked! He never saw her reading, she betrayed no interest in anything as far as he could see. She was just an animal, a great, big, stupid animal. But what if, after all, she *did* think? What if, after all, she *did* have a secret being? You could never tell from her face what she was thinking; but suppose, after all, she was living her own private, personal life behind that impassive mask of flesh. Perhaps, she had an individuality and could see visions and dream dreams. And did he have a part in those visions and those dreams? It was just possible that she despised him, that essentially he did not matter to her. The thought humiliated him; he felt snubbed, and the possibility of her tolerating him and humouring him like a child angered him more than any full-blooded hate would have done. If that were so, he would make her suffer as she had made him suffer. He would punish her, torture her painfully and slowly; he would goad her into speech until he knew what went on in her big, stupid head.

It was only by chance that Henry came to link up Mabel with Colin. He had been reading the paper as usual at the breakfast table, and Mabel must have been reading the page which was turned to her, because all of a sudden he felt her stiffen and when he looked over the top of the paper wall, he saw (or thought he saw) for the first time since their marriage the faintest sign of emotion in Mabel's face. He was certain that she had seen something in the newspaper that excited her. Something she had read, or perhaps it was a picture she had seen, had caused this sign of human feeling in her face. This was in the nature of a miracle to Henry, since he had already settled in his mind that his wife was merely animal. He was determined to find out what lay behind this sudden lighting up of his wife's face, but he was just as determined that he would find out without asking any questions.

Henry prided himself on his finesse. At first, he pretended he noticed nothing; then, when he escaped from the house to his desk at the office, he looked at the page which Mabel must have read and which must have contained the cause of her sudden excitement. The picture of a distinguished looking man, slightly grey at the temples according to the photograph, looked back at him. The caption said that he had just returned from the States and that his name was Dr Colin Giles. It seemed to Henry that the man had a sneer about his lips, and this fact, coupled with the infinitely more important one that he had neither seen nor heard of this man before, led him to the conclusion that he was the cause of Mabel's excitement. He pictured in every detail with which his feverish imagination supplied him the boy and girl love affair between Mabel and this man. Mabel had never mentioned his name, he argued, but he had always heard that girls never forgot their childhood sweethearts; and the fact that she had never called his name or even talked about an early boyfriend, was proof positive that there was something in it. But he would get to the root of it, if he had to die in the attempt. So that was why she was so calm and sedate, so poised, so serene. All the time she was living a romance in her mind. He, himself, was nothing to her. All the years she had been thinking of this Colin. How could he have been so blind? He had called her a fool, a dull, stupid animal. Well, it seemed that he had been the fool. But he was a fool no longer. He knew her secret now and he would hold it over her head until she came to her knees before him. He would humble her; she would see what good it did to exclude him from her thoughts. By God, he would show her!

During the months that passed, Henry saw a quickening in his wife. She seemed more sprightly, happier, radiant even. The more he thought about it, the more certain he was that his wife was unfaithful to him, if not in the flesh, in the spirit, and the more he thought about it, the more he felt that unfaithfulness of the spirit was much the more serious of the two. His suspicions, silent and suppressed, grew into a jealousy too big for him. But still he was patient until he thought (not giving her credit for being able to put two and two together) the time was ripe for him to mention Giles' name in a casual, careless sort of way. He would then watch for her reactions to confirm his suspicions. The plan was simple. She could never suspect that he suspected.

'Did you see that there's a new malaria specialist at the hospital?' he had asked yesterday morning at the breakfast table. 'He's from the States.' His tone had a studied casualness.

'Oh yes!' Mabel replied. Her reply was a half question and took its cue from the question itself. Henry gained no ground by his finesse.

'I wonder if he's a Trinidadian!' Henry said, expecting an answer. His strategy was more direct now.

Mabel did not answer at all and her silence irritated him. He could not bear to be ignored.

'Well, aren't you going to ask who he is?' he asked, surprised that his voice was uncontrollable and angry.

'Why?' Mabel asked. 'What does it matter to me?' She seemed genuinely surprised that he could think she would be interested in such a matter.

Henry could find no answer to her question.

'His name,' he said, 'is Dr Giles; Dr Colin Giles.' He let the name drop carelessly from him, with a sort of elaborate nonchalance, as a man drops a penny into a slot machine and secretly dares to hope that a million dollars will come out.

'Oh, yes,' she said, and there was no meaning, hidden or exposed, in the uninflected words.

Henry went to work in a savage mood. Defeat and frustration made him desperate and sullen. The day stretched out in a bewildering succession of small irritations; it was hot and the water cooler was not working; it was windy and the wind kept blowing the papers off his desk. When he reached home in the afternoon, he was in a violent temper.

All that had happened yesterday. When he reached home, the house was silent. The letter was waiting for him on the centre table near the bowl of red exora flowers. He read it but could find no connection between Colin Giles and Mabel. The house felt strange, and for the first time in his life, Henry learned that a man can miss anything, even a pain, to which he has grown accustomed.

Henry sat the the table and remembered his wedding. He remembered how he had been staring at the tiny shaft of sunlight burnishing the brass candlesticks on the altar, and for no reason there were tears in his eyes. Certainly his marriage, their marriage, had been nothing but a long farewell. Mabel was right. She had found the only words for it. He remembered how she came up the aisle with her slow, lumbering gait on her father's arm, he remembered her over-powdered face, and remembering, he forgot that once he had thought of her as an animal without wit.

. . . Call it, if you like, a long farewell . . . the words refused to leave his thoughts, and once more, Mabel figured as no ordinary woman, but a queen, magnificent in her six foot stature and dignity.

Casuarina Row

Elizabeth Godding was a mild-eyed little girl who lived among a swarm of sisters and two brothers, Courcey and James, down in the village near the market. She was as demure and as shy as a nun, but she had a ferocity of imagination and such a startling idiosyncrasy of speech that, although by the village will and testament she was my girl even before we were twelve, I was never able to guess from one moment to the unpredictable next what random arrangement of words would issue from her mouth. Nor was I ever able to imagine what went on behind the bland brow, what images paraded before those lambent eyes that in the middle of a sentence would go all vacant and far away.

Every Saturday morning, Elizabeth cam running up Breakneck Hill. She dashed around the side of the house past the fowl run, climbed over the railings of the front verandah and, panting as if she had just manoeuvred her escape from the darkest of dungeons, still demure, presented herself to Grandfather who sat in his rocking chair contemplating the sea and expecting her.

Grandfather greeted her exactly as he greeted adults, seriously and solemnly, his manner bearing no trace of condescension, rather, the faintest glow of delight that he should be the object of her faithful regard.

'Good morning, Elizabeth,' Grandfather said every Saturday morning, as if it had been years and not only a week ago that he had greeted her.

'Good morning, Elizabeth,' Grandfather said, taking from his pocket the silver-wrapped, cream-filled chocolate that was his Sabbath blessing.

'Good morning, Grandfather, thanks,' Elizabeth would cup her two hands together to receive the blessing whose bounty would threaten to overflow the space offered by a child's two hands. And then she would curtsey and, if I were not around, ask Grandfather for me.

'George,' Grandfather would shout, 'Elizabeth is here.'

And so Saturday would begin.

Grandfather had planted at the edge of the garden a line of casuarinas which were about three or four years younger than I was and about as high off the ground. Our Saturday, Elizabeth's and mine, would begin with a visit to the casuarinas. Immediately after she had eaten her chocolate, as if it were magic food, Elizabeth became Mrs Gullet and I, by the consent of my affection for her, Mr Gullet. The Gullets were fettered imagination which had made of the row of casuarinas a collection of families, each of which possessed its own singular, distinct and inviolate identity.

Mr and Mrs Gullet we were, an elderly couple rendered childless by the fact that our children were 'away' – a clever Elizabethan contrivance which permitted the receipt of countless letters from them, and thus, the exercise of a tireless imagination: snow twenty feet on the ground and fog so thick that you could cut it with a knife, and tall buildings and clothes never seen and accents and languages never heard in our Prospect corner of the world. Letters came from all corners of the world containing reports of every variety of adventure; train journeys, monuments, accidents, calamities, all products of Elizabeth's, Mrs Gullet's, vivid imagination.

Slowly, the Gullets, arm in arm and as genteel as adults, made their way from tree to tree, from house to house, family to family, to whom my Saturday wife Elizabeth had given the most original of names.

'Good morning, Mrs Bucket,' she greeted the slender tired-looking casuarina at the head of the row, at the same time nudging me into a proper good morning.

She was always apologising to a casuarina for my lack
of manners or my absentmindedness, saying that I had
her in barracks.

'He doesn't mean anything by it,' she said, 'but you
know what husbands give.'

And I would find myself murmuring an apology to a
tree and asking after the health of Mr Bucket and the five
little Buckets standing sedately in a row at their mother's
right hand. Mr Bucket was a fisherman and was never able
to be found at home; if he was not out in the boat, he
was in the rum shop, Elizabeth said that Mrs Bucket said.
But he was a kind and thoughtful friend and was always
making us presents of fish: there was hardly a Saturday
morning Elizabeth did not leave the Buckets with a bright
blue chub or a red snapper or a handful of flying fish in
her basket. But Elizabeth thought Mrs Bucket dull and
said that she was a numb drum. The first time I heard
her say the words, I thought that Elizabeth had lost her
way again in the treacherous overgrowth of her amazing
vocabulary, and I said that surely she meant humdrum.
Elizabeth gave me such a look of pity that there and then
I realised that a numb drum was really what she meant
Mrs Bucket to be – a particularly unexciting instrument
of the orchestra. Elizabeth said that Mrs Bucket was a
complainer and I had to take her word for it. Certainly,
more than once while they chatted and Elizabeth asked
how the children were getting on, I heard a thin wail
from Mrs Bucket which sounded almost like the whine
of the wind in a casuarina. Elizabeth never let Mrs B talk
too much; she herself always had to give the news of our
own children; George was on an expedition in Arabia,
and Lysander, the second boy, was winning olé after olé
in the bull rings in Madrid. We had a daughter named
Cleopatra who was studying to be a doctor, and was so
busy that she didn't have time to write very much, but she
was well when last we heard from her. Elizabeth said that
she didn't much like visiting the Buckets but, since they

lived at head of the road, she couldn't very well pass the house without saying hello.

'They would feel bad,' Elizabeth said, 'and it wouldn't look good.' And I agreed with her that we should not snub them, especially when we could put pot on fire in the certainty of a fish or two every Saturday morning. I believe Elizabeth thought there was something mischievous in my argument, for that was one of the times when she accused me of being opposite.

The Buckets' neighbour was Sophie the Grandduchess. That was the only name we, or rather, I, knew her by. Elizabeth probably knew more about her than she told me, for they were always whispering together and giggling like little girls. There was no Grandduke in evidence and Elizabeth and I naturally, were too discreet to ask. Sophie had a little daughter who, Elizabeth said, was a marchioness, but I never saw her. She was sickly and Elizabeth was for ever advising Sophie about cures, one of which was so startling that, even accustomed as I ought to have been to Elizabeth's fantasies, I could not help protesting.

'You must bathe the child in black molasses,' Elizabeth said, 'that's the best thing for what the child has.'

'Black molasses, I . . .' I began to argue.

'Yes, black, b–l–a–c–k, black molasses,' Elizabeth said firmly, so that there should be no doubt. And I shut up. I was always finding out that I knew nothing at all about the most ordinary things.

Sophie the Grandduchess, who always carried on her conversations with her arms akimbo, did not very much credit the efficacy of Elizabeth's prescription, and bluntly refused to try it on the grounds that it sounded to her like obeah, a piece of recalcitrance which nearly broke the friendship. When, on the following Saturday morning, Elizabeth asked after the Marchioness and was told that she was better and, thinking proudly that the recovery was the result of a bath in black molasses three times a day, she was furious (that is as furious as Elizabeth could get) when Sophie told her that she hadn't tried the recommended cure. Sophie, arms at hips and swaying slightly (Elizabeth swore that she could smell the rum on her breath) must have made some kind of offensive or sarcastic remark about native cures or bush medicine which, to tell the truth, escaped me. But the next thing I knew was that Elizabeth grabbed me angrily and, muttering something about people being ungrateful, you did your best for them and they didn't evaluate it, led me away from the house.

For a few Saturday mornings after that incident, we used to walk past Sophie's house without even a good morning, Elizabeth holding her head high in the air and I a little sheepish and ashamed of her unexpectedly crude manners.

Yet, all in all, Sophie was good fun and Elizabeth, when they were on speaking terms, used to spend what seemed like hours every Saturday morning chatting and laughing and carrying on, while a little way off and out of earshot I fretted in silence. Elizabeth said that she liked Sophie because she was uphazard, which I had the wit to understand was the very opposite of numb drum. From where I stood, I could barely hear Elizabeth's whispered gabble, as Sophie did not do much talking, but, when Elizabeth began to tell me the things she said and how lively she was, I had to change my opinion. Once, Elizabeth said, Sophie draped herself in potato vine leaves and danced a mazouk in the moonlight to the great delight of all the neighbours. Elizabeth's opinion was that, as Sophie was a noblewoman, she didn't have to care what anyone thought of her. Up till then, I had thought that noblewomen used to care a lot what people thought of them, but I came to learn later that Elizabeth was, as usual, right.

One Saturday morning as we left the Buckets, I saw Elizabeth dab her eyes with her handkerchief and noticed that she gave no sign that she was stopping to see Sophie.

I was fairly sure that they werent't going through one of their things, for I hadn't heard Elizabeth say anything about *that* Sophie. I was more than curious to know what had happened. Elizabeth kept looking furtively at the house as if she did not see Sophie standing there, arms akimbo as usual, and I wondered what I ought to have known.

'We are not stopping to say hello to Sophie?' I asked.

Elizabeth burst into tears. I asked her what was wrong, but I could not understand what she was saying between the sobs. After a while, she stopped crying and said that she thought I had known that the little marchioness had died and that Sophie had gone away.

Sophie's house did not stay empty for long, not for more than two Saturdays. One morning, as we passed what I thought was the empty house, I said that I wondered how long the house would remain shut up and Elizabeth asked me if I hadn't heard that someone was moving in the next week. I began to tell her that the only person who gave me news of the people in Casuarina Row was herself, but she didn't seem to understand what I was saying and I let it go. I asked her who was moving in, and she told me the story of Nick the Kick.

Nick, Elizabeth said, had lived in Panama for years and years and had a lot of money, but he was very mean. He had a reputation as a woman beater and lived alone, doing his own washing and cooking and cleaning, which, Elizabeth said, showed that he was not a noble man. All this news Elizabeth picked from the neighbours, for she refused to speak to Nick, who would be standing at his front door or sitting in the verandah when we did our Saturday morning round. Elizabeth said he had no manners and ought to speak to us first as he was the stranger. But Nick, who was a rough sort of person, did not observe these niceties. I tried to tell Elizabeth that the kind of person I guessed Nick to be wasn't likely to care very much whether she spoke to him or not. After three or four Saturday mornings, I began to feel silly passing Nick's house with him standing in full view, picking his teeth or whistling, or just standing and staring at us while we pretended that he didn't exist. So, one morning, I raised my arm and said, 'Hello, Nick.' And immediately, Elizabeth said, 'Hello, Nick,' and stopped.

If you had heard Elizabeth, you would not have believed that she had ever said what she had about Nick the Kick. She didn't give the man a chance to speak. It was all, 'I was going to stop in, but I was letting you settle first. There's always so much to do when you move house. We moved once and it was two years, two years before we settled. Not so, George?'

And as I nodded in support, all I could think was, 'Cool, Elizabeth, very cool!'

Nick must have fallen for Elizabeth's interest, because she went on talking to him, asking him about Panama and telling him that her eldest brother Courcey once had a friend there and that she herself had always wanted to see Panama and did he see where they made the hats? And Nick, whose tongue was said to be so foul that it wanted scrubbing with pot soda and carbolic soap, that same Nick who had no respect for women, Nick the Kick, was silent. Elizabeth overwhelmed him, clearly.

'And how do you like these latitudes?' she asked Nick.

I wondered if Nick understood what she meant and whether he was as confused as I was when she first used that word to me. But I said nothing, remembering that Elizabeth used to tell her friends that I was simple. I expect Nick understood, because I didn't hear him ask her what she meant. Elizabeth went on talking about the neighbours, telling Nick about the Buckets next door and about Sophie and her daughter and all the households along the road: the Outs and their swarm of children (Mr Out was a baker and Elizabeth said that the children were always covered in flour from head to toe); and the Yellow Lady, whom Elizabeth refused to call by her proper name and who lived by herself and, Elizabeth whispered, was a witch because she was in the habit of talking to herself; and in the last house, right at the very end of the road, Miss Providence, who was a Seventh Day Adventist, and whom we never saw since she was always at church when we passed by on Saturday mornings, but who always left us, wrapped in brown paper on her doorstep, a loaf of coconut bread she had made before sunset on Friday.

I grew impatient while Elizabeth recited all the gabble gossip of Casuarina Row into Nick the Kick's unexpectedly receptive ears.

'Come on now,' I said.

Elizabeth said goodbye to Nick and I heard her promise him to call around the next day.

When we moved off, I said, 'But tomorrow is Sunday, Elizabeth.'

At first all she said was, 'You're jealous,' and I was thinking about that when she said, 'Yes, I know tomorrow is Sunday, but I'm Mrs Gullet on Sundays, too.'

I thought her voice had an edge to it, but I couldn't let go. 'We never go out visiting on Sunday, you know that very well, Elizabeth Gullet,' I said. My world was upside down and I could not understand what had happened or was happening.

'But we can, if we want to, and if you don't want to, George Gullet, I can go by myself.' She sounded as if she was more than play-play angry and I made the thing worse by asking, 'Do you like Nick the Kick?'

'Don't be stupendous,' she said, but I didn't understand whether she meant I was stupendous to ask, or whether the likelihood of her liking Nick the Kick was so remote that the question was an absurdity. Whichever way it was, I reckoned that something had happened to put an end to the Gullets' Saturday morning calls.

'It is stupendous to believe that casuarinas are people,' I said.

Neither Elizabeth, Godding or Gullet, made any comment. But one of them, I don't know which, hooked her right arm in the crook of my left elbow with a sedate and proper gesture of affection, and I remembered that my right arm, the sword arm, had to be left free to draw in defence of my lady.

But it was Elizabeth Godding who, suddenly turning the full glory of her quiet grey eyes upon me, asked me, not at all in the tone of possession which was the one she used whenever or wherever I was involved, it was that Elizabeth who asked me, as if for once my answer to her question would be of some importance, 'George, do you love me?'

I told Grandfather about this and even he, wise as he was, was unable to fathom the depths of so innocent yet so terrible a question.

Nothing in my thirteen or fourteen years had prepared me for the profundities of this confrontation, for I recognised, foolish and uxorious as I was, that this was more than a question to which I could answer yea or nay, as Elizabeth would say. So I hesitated. I thought that the seriousness of the question deserved more than an impulsive answer. I thought: Nick the Kick, adolescence; whatever Elizabeth, Godding or Gullett, it didn't matter which, may have guessed me to be, I was not a complete fool. Why did she want to know? I said to myself, 'Now George, however you answer this question, you will be in the wrong. Think, think.' And I thought of all the Saturday mornings, the visits, the uneasy nonsenses, the play-play realities and, after all the thinking, I said, 'Yes, Elizabeth, I believe I love you.'

'Why did you have to stay so long to answer?' Elizabeth asked, and strutted off clutching her basket with the blue chub and the bonito Mrs Bucket had given us that morning.

Saturday morning came again and Grandfather sat in his rocking chair. It was long past ten o'clock and no Elizabeth had put in an appearance.

'No Elizabeth this morning, George?' he asked. 'I wonder what's wrong.'

And I, who had no secrets from Grandfather, did not wish to, did not know how to, say that the casuarinas he had planted were, jump high, jump low, only a row of trees.

Septimus

Mama is in tears with the letter in her hand, and I know that she has heard from Seppy. Mama always cries when she hears from Seppy, but at Christmas her tears have a special meaning. Mama's tears are now, and have been long before Seppy ever went to Canada, a part of our family's Christmas rites.

For Mama, there is no such person as Seppy. Our little brother, the last of us, may be Seppy to us, his sisters, but for Mama he has always been Septimus. 'Your father,' she has always insisted, 'called him Septimus because he was the seventh, and that is his name.' And so for the sake of the season, the six of us girls make a point of saying Septimus, just to please the old girl.

She is in tears. I take the letter from her hand and read it. Septimus has sent a 'little something' for her, but it is not this act of filial thoughtfulness that makes Mama cry. It is the last sentence of Seppy's Christmas letter: 'Tell the girls that at last I can have a whole apple for Christmas.' When I remember the origin of that sentence, I feel a little like crying too.

We have always lived in the Gap – a narrow lane between the canefields, just a little longer than a cricket pitch, although it seemed a boundless highway to us at the time I am now remembering. There were three houses in the Gap at this time, one belonging to old Bostic, the watchmaker, our own, and, at the far end, right on the edge of the canes, a ramshackle old gabled house, smelling of mice, mildew and camphor, where Aunt Bless lived.

The seven of us ruled the Gap. We shall never, however

rich we may become, ever possess anything as completely as we possessed the Gap.

It was ours, from the stones and potholes to the trees in each backyard, from old Bostic, grumpy, pulling his moustache, to old Bostic's cow, Blossom, which he put out to graze every morning before he left for his little shop in Bridgetown.

I don't think old Bostic really liked children, but there was nothing he could do about our ownership of him: he used to put up with us and made the best of it. Sometimes, he would even play his guitar for us, and, if he had a few drinks, he might even go so far as to yodel – a magnetic performance which made him seem wonderfully different from his tightly wrapped-up, lonely old self.

Aunt Bless was a willing, even eager, possession of ours. Her fruit trees, her garden, all the strange things in her front room – she had a what-not, an épergne, a cut glass decanter full of camphor water, and a collection of turban-like hats like those worn by Queen Mary – all of them belonged to us.

Even her name belonged to us, for it was Septimus who christened her Aunt Bless. Before he was born, we used to call her Aunt Letty (her name was Letitia), but as soon as he could speak, he called her Aunt Bless. Septimus was the first of us to notice that she never used the conventional greetings of 'Good morning' or 'Good evening'. It was always 'Bless you, Maisie' (to Mama) or 'Bless you, child', to one of us. Needless to say, Septimus was her favourite.

One Christmas Eve when the six of us girls were ready to go along to Aunt Bless with the basket of cake and ginger beer which Mama made for her every Christmas, Septimus, who must have been six or so at the time, did not want to go. He was in a bad mood.

Mama had not long before come back from town with her bag full of sweets and presents she had bought for us. There were packages of peppermints wrapped in shiny red paper, oranges, a tiny motor car for Septimus, hair ribbons for us girls in pink and yellow and blue, a big picture book for all of us, and three apples, red and rosy on the top of the bag.

Immediately he saw the apples, Septimus grabbed one of them and ran off. We all ran behind him and caught him under the breadfruit tree at the back of the house before he had time to do more than fondle the rich redness of the apple.

We dragged him back to the house howling and kicking. Mama gave him a lecture: 'No, Septimus,' she scolded, 'there are only three apples, and we must share them among all nine of us.' We all knew that our father would give Septimus his share, but the principle had to be established that what we had – which was not much – had nonetheless to be shared among all nine of us.

'I want a whole apple,' Septimus shouted in protest, too young to understand.

'You can't have a whole one,' Mama said, 'and that's that.' When Mama spoke, she spoke.

'And now,' she said, drying his tears with her handkerchief, 'you must stop crying and go with the girls up to Aunt Bless to take her her Christmas.'

Aunt Bless greeted us and hugged all seven of us, one after the other, overpowering us with the scent of Khuskhus root with which she perfumed her clothes, and murmuring, 'Bless you, child', with each embrace. She took the basket from Maria, the eldest (very lady-like on these occasions – 'playing Mama'), who had a protective arm around Septimus who was still snivelling.

'What's wrong?' Aunt Bless asked, concerned that her darling boy was not happy. 'What's wrong, Septimus? Tomorrow is Christmas!'

Septimus did not answer. He just stood there, fighting back the tears and looking foolish. But his feelings were too much for him and he blurted out between his sobs: 'I want a whole apple and Mama says No!'

Aunt Bless grasped the situation right away. She gathered Septimus to her, her own eyes now swimming with love and feeling, and she hugged him and kissed him and told him not to mind: that Aunt Bless would see that he got a whole apple, because he was her own little Septimus.

At last, Septimus stopped crying and Aunt Bless took him into her bedroom, where it seemed to us children that not even the sun went, and then we heard sounds of rummaging and scuffling as if Aunt Bless were turning out all the treasures of her hope-chest. And then Septimus's laughter pealed out as clear and silver as a bell.

Septimus came out of the darkness of Aunt Bless's room with his eyes shining bright and as big as saucers and clutching in his hand the biggest and rosiest apple I have ever seen.

All the way home, Septimus held his apple to his bosom. He said not a word to any of us. I think we were a little ashamed of him and the scene we made, and we knew that Mama would be angry with us for letting him accept the apple.

When we got home, Septimus ran to the kitchen and we hurried to tell Mama what had happened. All of us tried to talk at the same time, and it was not easy for Mama to get the story. But she did at last, and she was so angry that she did not speak.

She rushed out to the kitchen with all of us trooping behind her. But she was too slow, for Septimus met her at the kitchen door with a saucer in his hand.

'Bless you, children,' he said. 'Bless you, children.' And he handed Mama the saucer with nine slices of apple on it.

Alleluia Morning

'Good morning, Miss Morning.'

The voices, the village voices echo through the open window, through the early morning mist, past the tops of the skyscrapers and enter the room.

'Good morning, Miss Morning, Miss Morning, Miss Morning.'

The voices sing diminuendo, sing the morning as their owners, so many mornings ago, pass outside my mother's window and find the song in her name impossible to resist.

'Good morning, Miss Morning,' sang the men and women, the boys and the girls, big and small, in my village, in greeting; and now, hundreds of mornings after, high in a room in a great city where no one sings in greeting in the morning, I hear the singing voices again. They are always singing and I have only to pause and be still to hear them like rain hushing the trees far away or the sea sobbing against the shoulder of the shore.

I know no one with a name like mine. I have never heard of anyone called Morning, only my mother and me. I did not know my father, and when I used to ask my mother about him, all she would say was, 'My dear, he died one morning,' A conundrum, that reply, whose meaning is not yet clear.

'Your name,' my mother told me, 'is your name. It is Alleluia Morning.'

'What is your name?' my mother asked me, over and over, again and again. And again and again, I would have to say my name like a lesson learnt by heart, like the answer to two and two.

'Alleluia Morning,' I would say, 'Alleluia Morning is my name.'

'Sing it, child, sing it,' my mother commanded me.

And I sang my name, Alleluia Morning, every morning, noon and night. I sang my name as I used to hear everyone in the village singing it.

'Sing your name at the top of your voice,' my mother said to me. 'It is yours and no one can take it from you unless you want them to. It may be all you have, but it is yours.'

And I sang my name, Alleluia Morning, at the top of my voice. 'Why did you give me that name?' I asked my mother.

'Because I was glad when you were born,' she said. 'Because you were as welcome as a blessing, I cried "Alleluia" when you were born.'

I loved my name and used to sing it and hear it singing in my ears, and the sound of it made me glad because I was a blessing to my mother. And, in turn, there was never another name as beautiful as my name, and there was a time when I would feel sorry for the Glorias and the Dorothys and Helens and Joans and Josephines and Marys because their names were not as sweet as mine, Alleluia Morning.

When I was going off to school, my mother spoke to me again. She charged me not to lose my name.

'Your books, your slate, your pencil, the ribbons in your hair; lose them, throw them away if you like, but never play careless with Alleluia Morning. It is all that you have. Don't put it down carelessly and forget it, and don't let anyone play games with it, don't let anyone steal it from you.'

'And why,' I asked my mother, 'should anyone steal my name from me?' I laughed. I could not think what a person could do with a stolen name. But my mother was cross with me. She felt I was making fun of her.

'Because,' she said, when I had stopped laughing,

'because people are like that. They will steal it because they think it is too good for you, and after they have stolen it, they will throw it away, on the stuff heap, because they will not know what to do with it. And it will rust and rot so that in the end it will be of no use to you or to them.'

And I went off to school with my mother's warning ringing and my name singing in my ears, Alleluia Morning.

'Good morning, children,' my teacher said.

'Good morning, teacher,' the children sang.

'Names, please,' the teacher said.

And one by one, we sang our names to the teacher. Alice and Mary and Belle and Grace, Judy, Jenny, Germaine, Violet, Frances, Flavia, Doreen and Delcina and Flora and Eileen and Joyce and Maria. And then, 'Alleluia, teacher, Alleluia Morning.'

'What?' asked the teacher. She could not believe what she had heard. And so, remembering what my mother had told me, I sang my name, I sang it at the top of my voice.

'Alleluia Morning,' I sang.

'What a strange name,' the teacher said, and the girls giggled.

'I have never heard a name like that before,' the teacher said, and the girls giggled even more.

'Are you sure that's your name?' the teacher asked, and the girls burst out in giggles so loud that she could not hear me when I said that I was sure that it was my name, because my mother had given it to me.

'That's enough, girls,' the teacher said.

'Is that your real name?' she asked, quietly and in a very kind voice.

The girls were all quiet and listening when I told the teacher again that I was sure that my real name was Alleluia Morning, because my mother gave it to me when I was born.

'It is a very pretty name,' the teacher said. And I told her that I knew that it was pretty because my mother had warned me to be very careful with it and not to lose it, as it was all I had.

That day, the girls gathered around me in the playground.

'What is your name?' they asked.

'Alleluia Morning,' I said.

'Your real name?' They did not believe.

'Yes,' I crossed my heart and hoped to die, 'my real name.'

'Say it again,' they begged, 'we have never heard such a name before.'

And I sang my name as my mother had taught me. Over and over again, I sang my name.

'Alleluia Morning, Alleluia Morning.'

One girl said, 'Let us call her Allie. That's shorter and nicer.' And they all said together, 'Yes, let's call her Allie, that's shorter and nicer.'

I understood that they wanted to be friends, that they meant kindness and I nearly said, I was on the edge of saying, 'All right, I don't mind, you can call me Allie if you wish. That's shorter.' But then I remembered what my mother had told me, how she had warned me not to let anyone play games with my name, nor take it from me, nor rob me of any part of it. And so, although I know that my new friends meant kindness by calling me Allie, I said that my name was Alleluia and I would prefer it if they called me by my right name. And I told them what my mother had said that, when I was born, she was glad and said, 'Alleluia,' and that I was to take care of my name as long as I lived. And the girls laughed and one or two of them began to tease me by singing 'Allie, Allie, Alleluia, Allie, Allie, Alleluia,' but although I knew that they were not going to steal my name, I knew too that I had to be careful, for without meaning to, they might break my name, as sometimes I had broken a glass or saucer just through carelessness, and all I cried afterwards was never enough to mend the broken thing again. So, although I knew they meant no harm by their 'Allie, Allie, Alleluia,' I cried out to them.

'No, no,' I cried, 'my name is Alleluia, my name is Alleluia.'

'But we are only making fun' the girls said. 'We know your name is Alleluia. It is a very pretty name.'

'Then call me by my very pretty name,' I said.

And the girls said, 'All right, all right then, we'll call you by your name; but we were only making fun.'

'But you said,' I reminded them, 'that Alleluia is a very pretty name.'

'All right,' they said, 'Alleluia.'

My mother was right. I had to be on guard always. Oh, the tricks they used to try to rob me of my name.

The tricks of the devil, as my mother had told me. The girls meant no harm but the result would have been the same as if they had been malicious. I grew bigger and went to another school and there, at first, they tried to make me ashamed of my name so that I would put it away for myself. They called me Morning, Afternoon, AM, Forenoon, Foreday Morning, everything but my real name, Alleluia Morning! It was not easy. Many times, I was tempted to forget my mother's charge and say, 'Let them call me whatever they like. They can't change the real me. I am what I am. After all, what's in a name?' But I always heard my mother's voice singing "Alleluia" in my ears.

'Sing your name, sing it out at the top of your voice.' My mother's voice rang out, 'You are a blessing and I called you Alleluia.' And, hearing my mother's voice, I would be strong enough to turn on the temptation and say, 'My name is Alleluia Morning.'

And gradually, always after I had shown how stubborn I was over my name, stubborn and over-sensitive and wearing a chip on my shoulder and all the other fancy words they gave to my simple wish to be called by no other name than the name my mother gave me, reluctantly they would give in and say, 'All right then, your name is Alleluia Morning.'

The tricks were legion. What kind of a name is that? A peasant name, a name from the backwoods, a slave's name, a name without sophistication, a made-up name, a false name, no name at all. But the subtlest, the cleverest trick of all was played when I came to this great city to study and to sing.

'Oh!' they cried, 'Alleluia Morning, what a beautiful name!' Tutor, music master, professor, accompanist, all of them, with one voice, cried, 'What a beautiful name!' They clapped their hands, delighted, and said, 'A beautiful name to match a beautiful voice.'

And I was glad that at last, far from home, strangers recognised how beautiful my name was. I was happy and said to myself, 'I could live here contented forever among these kind people who are so quick to see and acknowledge how beautiful my name is. They are truly what they say they are, civilised and cultivated and humanist and without prejudice and may indeed be the chosen people of heaven.' I was so happy that I sang like a bird, from recital to recital and from concert to concert. From town to town, all over the country, from shore to shore, my name sang, Alleluia Morning. The headlines of newspapers carried my name, the radio sang it, the records multiplied and everywhere I went, I heard myself singing. I sang like a blessing, like a bird, they said, and I was happier than I had ever thought I should be.

Moreover, my mother, far away, was happy too. She wrote each week to tell me what a gladness it gave her that I was singing in the big country and that I was truly a blessing. She heard my voice sometimes, and she was so happy when she did that she could not help crying. But she warned me, she would never grow tired of warning me, I was never to forget to guard my name: I was not to be careless with it. Remember, she wrote, remember and have a care.

Last night, I sang before the greatest crowd of all, in the greatest hall in this great city. Rows and rows of people sat before me, and when I sang for them they shouted, they clapped their hands and cried 'Bravo, bravo!' at the tops of their voices. And I sang again and again and yet again; and the more I sang, the more they wanted me to sing. In the end, when, unwillingly, they stopped clapping and went away, I sat in the dressing room before the mirror, among the red roses and the yellow roses and the gladioli and all the many coloured flowers of tribute and triumph. Admiration was all around me. I felt myself floating on the voices of congratulation, high above the hands outstretched to touch, the programmes offered for autographs, the adoration, the sweet adoration. And the newspaper critics, the music men, all flattering and courteous. I knew them all. They had all been kind to me for many years and many concerts, and some of them had predicted that one day I should have such a success as this. I knew them all except one. There was a young, fresh-faced, handsome one, with the whiskers of the moment's fashion and a furtive smile curving around the corners of his mouth. I had never seen him before.

He caught me looking at him. 'Miss Morning,' he said, offering his hand in greeting, his eyes also offering his tribute of praise and congratulation, 'that was the finest singing I have ever heard.'

I thanked him. 'I have to write it up,' he said, 'and I don't know what to say.'

I was touched. I had never, I thought, been paid such a compliment.

'But, tell me, Miss Morning,' the young man was saying, 'I hope I don't seem rude, but is your name really Alleluia Morning?'

'Yes,' I said, after a while, a long while, 'it really is.'

'Thank you, Miss Morning.' The young man bowed politely and turned on his heels and shoved his way through the throng to the door.

The newspapers carry my picture this morning and my name is in headlines. Alleluia Morning, the newspapers shout, a triumph! A voice like a blessing! A glad voice! The banners scream.

Below one headline my eyes catch the words: ". . . continues to insist that her real name is Alleluia Morning. If it is, then never was a name more proper."

My mother was right, is right. You cannot be careless, there are all sorts of tricks to rob you of your name.

Meeting in Milkmarket

Thirty-five years ago, George Sampeter and I sat in the same class next to each other in the elementary school. We were friends, by which I mean that he was easy with me and I liked him and was easy with him. You will see that I am using "friends" in the sense in which I would have used it as a child, innocently and trustingly. Now, before I use the word, I must, as it were, look behind my back. I must ask myself whether the thing that exists deserves the name, whether I am not perhaps claiming too much. But I was less cautious when George and I walked together from school and shared sugar cakes and fish cakes, and I did not question whether the thing that we shared could justify its claim to the title of friendship.

Today I met George in the Milkmarket after more than 30 years. The thing that strikes me now is my own reaction to meeting him after so long. From day to day, I often see men who went to school with me and who have, in the common way of speaking, done well for themselves. They are now doctors and lawyers, some of them, politicians and high-up civil servants, and one of them is the Chief Justice, a knight and Counsel of the Queen. Sometimes, depending on the propitiousness of the occasion, the time of day or night, the place and the surroundings, the degree of sobriety, they see me too and nod a greeting or avert their eyes to a shop window as the case may be. Whenever I encounter one of these people, I always feel a burning angry shame and self-contempt. and invariably that day or night, I contrive to get quite drunk. Nowadays, I get drunk much too often. They know not what they do, these people. And this is why I am not afraid to say that George was my friend, is my friend, for seeing him has left me happy and glad in a choking way that I was at school with him, glad for myself, and somehow simply and unambiguously rewarded by the memory that, when we were children, I shared in his life and experiences.

I remember very clearly the morning that George came to school for the first time. He was late and prayers had already been said when his father led him through the school room to the headmaster's desk on the platform. I could see that he was frightened by the way he held on to his father's hand, and I felt a trifle sorry for him that he needed a hand to clutch for support in what seemed to me no great ordeal. I think now that there was also in me a little envy of his fortune in having a father's hand to clutch. The headmaster greeted George's father warmly, and it was clear that they were friends and that George would be one of those boys who would get special treatment, being the son of the head's friend. That made me angry, I remember. What made me even more angry was that George was put straight into the second standard. This seemed a monstrous piece of favouritism. But it did not last long. By the next morning, George was among us humbler folk in the first standard: he could read very well and on this basis had been put into the class above, but the teacher soon found out that George couldn't do sums. As this was considered superior to all other skills, George had to be demoted. They put him to sit next to me. He was crying from the public shame. I wanted to comfort him, but I could think of no way of doing it. He had a new slate and a new pencil which for some reason would not write. I had an old cigarette tin full of pencil ends (in all my school days I never had a whole pencil) and I gave him one and showed him how to lick the tip with his tongue to make it write. We became friends from that moment and I have never ceased to be proud of myself for that simple gesture. I have done nothing in my life since which has pleased me more.

George came from the country, and brought with him a sense of wonder and thrill at the sights of town. Our school was a slum school in the heart of the dirty back streets, littered with fruit skins, reeking with the "fainty-fainty" smell of rotten and rotting fruit. In the doorways of Suttle Street, the patois-speaking mesdames from Dominica and St Lucia watched over barrels of mangoes and sacks of charcoal. All sorts of spices spread a perfume in the air, and the girls of the town, their mouths filled with gold and curses, slutted and strutted along the narrow wet street. George loved it all. I did not; I lived in it. After school, every afternoon, I would try to persuade George to take the road by way of the waterfront so that we might look at the schooners and the bare-backed seamen smoking on the decks or fishing over the sides: the smell of the sea offered a more promising and certainly cleaner prospect than the one that hedged me round in Suttle Street. But the dirt and the muck fascinated George: the sacking curtains that screened the beds from the street, the smoky oil lamps, the half-starved dogs, kicked from one end of the road to the other. He would spend an hour listening to the patois shouts and curses that flew across the street, and so miss the bus.

George, in those days, had a country boy's simplicity and lack of guile, and I prided myself on my sharpness, my knowledge of the back streets and the ways of the city. I showed off to George and he rewarded me by finding everything I showed him fascinating.

My mother made our living by taking in washing and selling sugar cakes and fish cakes at the door of our house. As I have said, after school in the afternoon, I was always reluctant to take the road past our house on our way to George's bus. It is easy to say that I was ashamed and did not want George to see where I lived, but this would have been true only at first. It was more than that, I think. Suttle Street was a dirty, filthy place. It was never clean. I lived there because I had no other place to live, but I hated the place. But there was another reason for George's eagerness to pass by my house which I never suspected. It was my mother who told me one evening when I came home alone that she thought that he was fond of my sister, Florianne. Like so many other facts, as soon as I had been told, I recognised this as true beyond question and could not understand how I could have failed to see it before. George could draw very well and he was forever filling his drawing book with sketches of Florianne and asking me to give them to her. As far as I remember, he never spoke more than a few words to her when they met on the road before or after school. Florianne went to the girls' school next to the church, and since this was on our way home, she had to dawdle to make sure of meeting us. Others besides my mother had noticed it too, and very soon George became the victim of some very cruel teasing from the boys which led, in the end, to the end of the affair, such as it was.

I find it now very difficult to say all this. First of all, it happened such a long time ago and then, although in my memory it seems big and important and to contain the distillation of our time and place, yet I have a misgiving that it is pitiably trivial and not worth the weight which my own heart seems to give it. And yet I know that I was right, and that the trivial events of 30 years ago opened my eyes to the realities. It has always amused me when people refer to sexual and biological matters as the facts of life and imply that the child who has been made aware of them is no longer to be thought of as a child. But the true facts of life are hardly so simple. The mating of male and female and the resulting production of animal life, these in my experience hold less mystery and need far less explanation than the conventions and artificialities which we have erected to separate one man from another. Yet no one explains or tries to explain these facts of life to a child, who is left to blunder against closed doors, to fumble with false combinations and finally to wander forever in a bewilderment from which neither age nor future experience ever succeeds in rescuing him.

The teasing of the boys was not malicious, and yet I cannot be sure. Perhaps, after all, it was more than a simple recital of the facts, and contained more recognition that any conceivable affection between George and my sister upset some sort of balance and did not fit into a desirable scheme of things. It was not that our schoolfellows were more than normally class conscious in any crude way, but they reacted in the only way they knew to an incongruity which they recognised immediately. They laughed, and chanted, 'Georgie like a barefoot girl.' They saw no irony in the fact that several of them wore no shoes themselves. They repeated the chant at every opportunity until the simple fact became a taunt, then an accusation, and then something like a savage curse. I can hear it now, the ringing, almost triumphant, 'Georgie like a barefoot girl,' as three or four boys trail behind George and myself as we turn the corner by the church and the girls' school. The words seem to tell the total story of our society. They need no explanation, they stand by themselves as a monument to the crassness of human thinking, the grossness of our sentiments and the thoughtless, awful cruelty of our behaviour.

'Georgie like a barefoot girl.' The chanted refrain echoes in my memory, and even now I can feel the helpless anger which flooded me. I was helpless, but George was both helpless and frightened. He had never experienced anything like it and his patent terror made me take what action I could to help him – action that showed how ignorant I was of the ways of the adult world.

One morning, George came as usual to wait for me while I got myself ready for school. As he waited outside in the street while I swallowed my breakfast biscuit, four boys turned the corner by the grocery. George sensed that they would begin their usual chant and tried to escape by diving into our front room. But he could not escape, and when I came out of the back room, I found him cornered like an animal while the four boys chanted the usual words. My mother was not at home, but Florianne was, and I could hear her sobs as she tried to stifle them by burying her head in the bedclothes. George and I were followed all the way to school by the cruel refrain.

I went straight to the headmaster, thinking in my innocence that as he was the friend of George's father, he would at least find some sort of suitable rebuke for the boys. What he did was much simpler. He summoned George and told him that he must stop at once his practice of walking along Suttle Street. There were other roads, he said, decent roads which George could take. He also told George's father some version of the story for, from the following morning, someone always accompanied George to school and came in the afternoon to collect him. That was the end of our walks through town, our idlings by the waterfront and the shop windows, the end of something which had hardly begun, but which we had shared, the end of any promise which our friendship had seemed to hold. It was not long after that George left the elementary school and our paths ceased to cross.

Today, it seems strange that in all the in-between years we never so much as spoke to each other: we might just as well have been in different worlds. I did see George some years after, when he was about sixteen, playing cricket for his school. When he came to bat, my heart was in my mouth for him, but he could not know that I was in the crowd. And then I heard that he had gone abroad, and that was all.

Today, he saw me before I saw him. His voice has not changed very much; it had always been deep. He shouted to me from the other side of the street, and when I heard my name, I turned to see him smiling. I was pleased as a child; I can't say how pleased I was. He shook my hand and asked how I was. His voice was careful and controlled. I could not answer. My clothes, the shiny old trousers, spoke for themselves. He was confident, assured, in a sports shirt and light cotton slacks and open-toed sandals, like a tourist. It was good to see him and to be remembered by him. And then a cloud crossed his face and he said, 'Stanley, it's been a long time. I am glad to see you, but I must run.' 'Yes', I said. I understood. He let go of my hand while he spoke, and after he left me, I stood watching his figure mingle with the crowd in the Milkmarket.

But what I cannot understand is why, as he was leaving, I should have said to him, to George, my friend, 'Goodbye, sir.'

The Old Man and the City

I had been living in Port-of-Spain for six years when I met the old man whose personality is now, 30 years after, inseparable from the personality of the city. To be sure, I had heard stories of an old fellow living on the left bank of the Dry River who had amassed, no one knew quite how, the finest collection of classical music on records on (the particular preposition is a clue to the source of the stories) the island, and who was an amateur, in the original and proper sense of that mismanaged word, of antique furniture, bric-à-brac and rare china. But the personality evoked by the stories I had heard was of a mild eccentric, a kind of legend, and since I was then still a victim of the belief that the finest spirits dwelt in the past, it was not difficult to persuade myself that the old man did not really exist in the here and now. And what gave massive support to the incredibility of the old man's actual existence was the singular provenance of the stories. For the wonders of rare pieces, cherished albums, old books and photographs and meticulously arranged records came to me, not through the native picong, but through the grapevine of a number of people who used, in those days, and possibly even more so now, to be referred to, with pejorative condescension, as expatriates, as if the population of the city was not itself overwhelmingly expatriate in origin. But, although in time I came to see that this expatriate awareness of the old man's presence was only one of the stunning contradictions which were the city's idiom, all the same time it seemed distinctively odd that it should fall to aliens to spread the gospel of a living native wonder. The fact that I know much better now is due as much to the lesson of the old man as to any other experience of life in the city.

Inevitably then, there was a mythical quality associated with the personality I encountered, in the final event not quite by accident, yet haphazardly, one evening when Cecil Herbert took me, as a special treat and an earnest of his regard for me, to a house off South Quay to meet a friend of his.

Tiptoeing up the front steps of the tiny house, as much in discretion as out of concern for the fragility of the floor boards, we waited for a while, then pushed a rickety half door to the box-like verandah. Cecil knocked and shouted, 'Clem!' in his deep-throated voice, which had first caught my ear in its recital of some lines which spoke of "far days in happy shires" and "goddesses caught in alabaster". An old man's voice, slightly quavering, answered: 'Who's that? Cecil?' as if Cecil's was precisely the voice which was expected at that moment.

When he appeared at the door clutching his pyjama trousers, the old man said, in a mock show of displeasure, 'Cecil, you old rogue, you wouldn't come to look for your friend all these months. What I do you?' But he was pleased by the visit, by the token of remembrance, and no one could be fooled by his tone into thinking that he was angry. Cecil was, of course, delighted and flattered – how could he not be? – by the tribute, and I was touched by the fondness in the old man's voice for "the old rogue".

Cecil introduced me and Clem slapped me on the shoulder in the off-hand gesture which, during the years I had lived in Port-of-Spain, I had come to recognise as not slighting nor rude, but as an invitation, an acceptance in an ambit of acquaintance and intimacy. For one brought up in the less casual environment of Barbados, where manners were more formal, the first encounter was unforgettable.

'But I don't see you, Cecil. I ask for you. I don't hear a word. What's happening?'

The concern was patent, anxious; but Cecil shrugged his shoulders, took a cigarette from a package, tapped it tight, lit it and blew the smoke through his teeth. The old man made a waving gesture to tell me that I had the freedom of the room and could sit where I liked, and I sat on an old mahogany sofa with a carved back of the period which I thought of as "Barbados plantation". Cecil settled in an armchair next to a glass-fronted bookcase, and the old man sat in what was clearly his favourite chair with his back to the door which led out to the yard. Between us, no more than an arm's length from either of us, in the centre of the triangle was the record player, its connecting wires hanging from a socket which swung from the roof, the focal point of the room, like a fireplace in a cold climate, the spot which engages the attention of all eyes.

The room was small and so crowded with bits and pieces that it was clear that movement about it was neither intended nor encouraged. How to describe it now, 30 years after the first impression? But the impression has faded very little. It was an old curiosity shop, cluttered with an accumulation of bijouterie and furniture, faded photographs in old but still elegant frames, a stately épergne, a crystal punch bowl and, locked behind another glass-fronted cupboard, several china cups and saucers; wine glasses on long stems as graceful as the necks of swans, silver teaspoons, a brass gong, four handsome pewter mugs, a gold snuff box, a crimson flower vase shot with mauve and indigo, a hand mirror with an embroidered back, a lady's sewing box, thimble and all, several pieces of jade, a glass egg. A trinity of candlesticks stood on top of the bookcase, flanked by an assortment of miniature china fixtures: little pigs, the Mad Hatter, Humpty Dumpty, Mr Pickwick, John Bull. In the corner of the room, alone on a triangular shelf, stood a handsome oil lamp with a brass bowl and a flowered chimney and a milk-white shade.

But I did not see all of this on that first visit. The

whole display was so unexpected that it was impossible to take it in at once, especially as there was only a dim light – Clem did not like bright lights, they hurt his eyes – which shone over the record player and left the room in dark shadow outside the edge of the circle of light. But there was enough light to see the outlines of photographs, hundreds of them on the walls, of artists and musicians and politicians and philanthropists. I could make out the rugged outlines of Albert Schweitzer's face, Ralph Bunche, Eve Curie. Over the doorway, presiding, there was a full length of Paul Robeson. There was Haile Selassie as well as George Washington Carver, Booker T Washington, George Headley, Ella Fitzgerald, Menuhin, the plaster cast of Paderewski's hands, Gershwin, Joe Louis, a wild-haired Albert Einstein.

Clem saw me looking around the room and said, 'You must come again whenever you like, now that you know the place. I am here all the time; too old to move around much now, eh Cecil?' And he chuckled hoarsely as if he and Cecil had shared the escapades of youth and as if the loss of that youth was the most amusing thing in the world. He spoke again in the unpretentious, easy-going manner that I was to come to know very well, which made the most generous act of hospitality, the most thoughtful kindness seem to be of no account, to be one of those everyday things that just happen.

'You boys would like a drink? I have some red wine there, had it since Christmas, keeping it for an occasion. And what is the use of a bottle of wine if you can't share it with your friends? But I can't vouch for it, so don't blame me if it tastes like vinegar.'

He chuckled again, this time at the monstrosity of the idea of wine tasting like vinegar, like a child, hugely and with a child's innocent delight. He brought out the wine, a dust-covered, unlabelled bottle, uncorked it with a fancy corkscrew and took three glasses from the cupboard. He wiped the glasses with a piece of toilet paper, pinged each one on its rim with the nail of his forefinger to show the quality, and handed one to each of us.

'Your health, gentlemen,' he said, with a hint of a bow in our direction as he sat back in his chair. We sipped. He said, 'Chambré,' chuckling again so warmly that I felt a glow of pleasure from his being so pleased. In the dimness of the room, I could not see his face, but it was impossible not to feel the cosy, warm-hearted welcome of his expression. We sipped in silence in the shadowed darkness of the room, the glow of the single bulb just enough to pick out the record player.

After a while, Clem asked, 'What about some music?' He sounded solicitous, eager to atone for having omitted so essential an element of hospitality. But, as I came to understand him later in our friendship, he was also showing off a little. He wished to offer his passion for our admiration, for if there was the slightest conceit in him, if he had the tiniest shred of vanity in his character, it lay in his collection of gramophone records.

'What about some music?'

Cecil turned and nodded, conceding to me, as new boy, the privilege of choosing.

The albums, hundreds, perhaps thousands of them, rested neatly on shelves around the room. I was at a loss to make a choice, like a child in the treasure house of a toy shop, surrounded by too many possibilities, too many realisable dreams. And, like a child, I tried to shift the onus of choice somewhere else.

'What have you got?' I asked, stupidly.

'What would you like to hear, man?' Clem's voice was a trifle sharp, I thought. I was being put on my mettle. In the gentlest manner, I was being asked how I dared to insult the occasion by not having an immediate preference. What kind of person was this that Cecil had inflicted on him? A man who did not even know what music he liked? I began to feel uncomfortable, and made a pretence of racking my brain for the piece of music that would be appropriate to the evening's mood, my own first visit, and at the same time convey the subtlest of suggestions that I did have a confident and developed taste in music. And, as it oftens happens when make believe exerts its demanding influence on our imaginations that we discover in the farthest recesses of memory, hidden under layers of much that is worthless but is hoarded against the possibility of its coming in handy some day, some unsuspected semblance of truth or reality, a forgotten experience came to my rescue.

A few years before, at a concert in Port-of-Spain, I had heard a visiting pianist play Debussy's *L'après-midi d'un faune*. More by instinct than through any refinement of musical appreciation I had enjoyed what I could think of only as the chordal assembly which seemed to me to convey exquisitely the suggestion of the title, which itself had caught my fancy. I had never heard this music before nor had I heard it since that evening but, suddenly, its sound came welling up on a wave of memory and I found myself asking a self-conscious question.

'Do you have *L'après-midi d'un faune?*'

Clem laughed out loud in ridicule, but not altogether unkindly, for it was the kind of naive question which gave him just the chance he wished to display the richness of his collection. He did so as modestly as his pride in his possessions would let him.

'Played by?' he asked.

He had me there. My ignorance lay exposed. But I dodged behind a façade of polite concession to the host.

'Who is your favourite?' I asked.

'Come on, the choice is yours. Say.'

Again, the surge of a faint recollection: of Claudio Arrau playing Chopin, a brilliant tone. Perhaps he had recorded Debussy. I took a chance.

'Claudio Arrau,' I said, with a little smugness in the fact that I knew the name of at least one famous pianist.

Without a word, Clem rose from his chair, went to a

shelf and, feeling with his fingers in the light that was too dark to see by, put his hand on the jacket of a record. He pulled out the record, puffed his cheeks and blew away the unseen dust and put the record on the player. He touched a switch and Debussy by Arrau poured into the room. No word passed until the end of the playing, and then Clem laughed in satisfaction. I murmured a word of unnecessary thanks.

We left the house that night about midnight. I was drunk as much with wine as with the elation of discovery, and as I was going through the door, thinking how to say that I would be back for more, Clem said, 'But, eh, eh, John, you have to sign the book. You know that when you go to Government House, you have to sign the book; what makes you think that you don't have to sign the book here too?'

And he pushed a heavy leather-bound book into my hand, made me find the page appropriate to my birthdate and sign of the zodiac and write my name to record my first visit.

The affection which came to life between Clem and me on and after that first visit was possible, I fancy, only because I had, by the time of its occurrence, already become familiar with the accent and idiom of the conundrum which was Port-of-Spain. That instantaneous affection, I have come to see, was itself a catalytic factor in any further understanding of the city that I may have achieved and so, old man and city stand in a relation to each other of mutual revelation and dependence. The idea of neither exists for me separately from the other; each of the two personalities promotes and illuminates the other precisely through the improbabilities of their association. Their co-existence within the same context of time could not have been imagined, but I came to see that the coincidence was of the same order of magnificence as those accidents which our hindsight eventually discerns to have been inevitable.

It was very near to where Clem lived, only across the road in fact, that I had had my first impression of Port-of-Spain. The bustle of the railway station, taxi drivers bawling invitations to travel to San Fernando, the dazzle of the bright lights of South Quay were more than the wartime economies of Bridgetown, from which I had only an hour or so before arrived, and the rural somnolence of Grenville, the only other town with which I had up to then achieved any measure of familiarity, had prepared me for. Port-of-Spain, Trinidad. Trinidad, Trickidad. Trinidad is a very nice place, but fire down dey. A schoolfellow, having following the trail laid by the Yankee dollar during the war, had returned and whispered into my uneasy ear that you could get anything in Trinidad. Anything, he had said ominously and had then added the rider, to buy. It was enough to frighten my timid spirit. And shortly before I had left my small island, a man who had studied these things told me that Port-of-Spain had for the Bajan the same combination of horror and fascination that a snake has for most people: it terrifies you, but you can't take your eyes off it.

And yet, the reality of the place turned out to be less than frightening. Congenial, easy-going, undemanding, purposeless (the most popular reason for any action or gesture or decision seemed to be "for so"), the atmosphere was the most accommodating it was possible to imagine. There was something for everyone. Although the Yankee had surrendered the freedom of the city to the then fledgling Sparrow, and the streets swarmed with their stranded "sufferers", there was still more money around than there had ever been in Bridgetown and there was little evidence of any reluctance to spend it, so that, compared to the town I had just left, Port-of-Spain had the appearance of un unbelievable bazaar, a big city *en fête*. And, even in places where there was no money, for there were pockets of poverty and neglect, the atmosphere of the city had bred a style which was undistinguishable from the style of high living. People greeted each other with shouts across the streets in terms of a picong which came perilously near to the edge of insult. But all was good-natured fun, which only a solemn, humourless Bajan would take exception to; and if you were disposed to look hard or listen carefully, you would have very little difficulty in persuading yourself that all was well. It was impossible to resist the appeal to jettison sobriety and to put an end to wartime self-denial.

And then there was the phenomenon of Carnival, for which there could have been no adequate preparation or apprenticeship. All that colour and explosion of high spirits, that abandon, that magnificent casting out of inhibitions were, in a jargon that had not yet been invented, something else. The world that was revealed was wonderful. There was a naked honesty about the expression that was refreshing and could not fail to capture the imagination, that was so attractive that it tended to assume a significance which a more sophisticated articulation would have denied. "For so" did not seem to be a satisfactory explanation.

And so it happened that what made the city infinitely more affecting was the transparency of the façade of sophistication. Pretty girls stepped smartly, primly sometimes, along Frederick Street pavements wearing their modish clothes with Parisian elegance and with just that touch of carelessness and nonchalance which, however natural it looked, was the result of a careful strategy to make sure that attention was never distracted by the clothes from the figure they clothed. The picture of one of them, a Junoesque beauty, a peau cannelle, walking down Marine Square licking an ice cream cone refuses to take leave of the memory. Saga Boys exaggerated the zoot suit styles, eager to make a pappy show of themselves in the name of fashion. It was when they came to speak, these boys and girls, that the innocent stranger felt that he had been taken. An English visitor, a painter

who lived in Barbados, described some of the girls as
"frothy". Extensive quotation of the Fitzgerald translation
of Omar Khayyam was regarded as the height of erudition.
The words of the serious calypsoes were of an unexpected
banality. It was disappointing. Style was everything. You
had to have it. For years, one had seen visiting Trinidad
cricketers display in Barbados the kind of style that was
now in evidence in Port-of-Spain. Bright, flamboyant
blazers and accents, a loose-limbed swaggering gait were
the features of their promenades along Broad Street. Only
our own Derek Sealy, with his knotted neckkerchief and his
cap daringly askew could match them for panache, and it
wasn't very long before he too went to live among them.

And yet, it was undeniable that the place was a joy. The
girls were decorous as well as decorative, the tram car
clanged along Frederick Street and around the Savannah
up to St Ann's and Bridgetown offered nothing as appeal-
ing as the pastime of sucking oranges and oysters on the
pitchwalk or as delicious as hot roti from the roadside trays
at the corner of Park and Charlotte, or as subtly flavoured
as pow from the Chinaman at the top of Queen Street.
And shallow as the talk might be, it was sharp and new
every morning. A tess was smoke, full of flash and grand
charge if he was not to be taken seriously, and if you tried
to stop a Trinidadian from "playing mas" you would be
spinning top in mud. You greeted your friend in the street
by giving him a right or giving him tone but if you wanted
to cut him dead, you passed him like a full trolley bus. It
was exciting and who cared if it was not profound? Life
itself lasted very little longer than the Red House fire, and
solemnity would not change the price of cocoa. Every year,
new kings and queens and knaves took over a new carnival
in a new profusion of colour. You could never grow tired
of the songs and the costumes and the picong. Until Killer
and Attila died and carried their styles with them. And one
Carnival Tuesday evening, after the city had lost its life, in
the dust and torn tinsel and the litter of broken bottles,

a pretty girl unmasked, her costume in tatters and she in tears that made channels through the paint on her face, cried as she scraped along St Vincent Street, barely able to lift her feet from the ground now that there was not a ping-pong of steel within earshot, cried to break her heart: 'Oh God! Never again, never again!'

Suddenly, Carnival stopped being the bright novelty it was trumped up to be and became the most traditional, the most conservative of fêtes, an annual redeployment of old ideas and conventions that had happened before and would happen again.

Precisely at this time of revelation, Clem entered my Port-of-Spain and I made my first entry into the unlikely world of his house at South Quay, and through it into a fuller understanding of the city. Given the happiness of that coincidence, it was no wonder that Clem, the man and his house and interest, assumed the dimension of a miracle. And even now, so long after the event, the sense of miracle persists, for it is clear that if I had not met Clem, and at that time, I should have been restricted to only the barest minimum of comprehension of the city, and that my appreciation of it would have been unable to withstand the assaults which time and events have made on its image. As it is, thanks to Clem, the place achieved a hard core of meaning which the Federation collapse, the politics of the post-1956 years, the "revolution" of 1970 and the oil boom have not been able to disfigure. In fact, much of what has happened since our meeting has served merely to confirm the meaning of Port-of-Spain as Clem led me to discover it. One incident which occurred at that time became part of the same package of experience which helped to make the picture of the city whole. It seemed at the time to be a duplicate of the meeting with Clem with which it combines to make a statement of the place where both occurred.

Paramin is a small village on the slope of the hill, behind the trees you can see across the Maraval valley to your left when you are on the road to Maracas. It has managed, partly because its attractions are not blatant, to escape the depredations of the now-for-now developers. The village centre comprises the wooden building which serves as school during the week and as church on Sunday, a shop and parlour and a standpipe and, from this huddle of communal elements, houses straggle up the hillside on one side of a beaten path which runs through the abandoned cocoa. Behind the houses, the hill slopes sharply down to a wide valley, but not too sharply to accommodate the beds of succulent chives for which the district is renowned.

We had heard that Paramin was one of the few villages in Trinidad remaining unspoilt, and we should still find there remnants of the charm and character which were so fascinating a feature of the old folks' stories. We had heard, in fact, that in Paramin we should hear very little English, and even that little would carry the old-time accent of the French patois which is the mother tongue of the village. But if we wanted to catch some of this old flavour, we should have to hurry, for no one knew how much time was left to the old customs and manners before they were taken over by galloping progress. And so, four of us set out one Sunday morning just before the rainy season began, when the pouis were still in flower, to make an expedition to the heights of Paramin.

When we arrived at the foot of the hill, mass had just ended and the villagers were coming out of the church and beginning to make their way back to their houses up the hill. Girls and boys, shy and eager, stared at us and returned our hellos with radiant smiles. Father greeted us from the door of the church when we parked the car. Port-of-Spain was barely twenty minutes away, but already we were in another world of bare feet, rustic courtesy and modest manners; a far, far cry from the strident brashness of Woodbrook and St James.

We set off up the hill along the path under the cocoa and the shading mango. Over to the right, the tree-filled valley stretched to the main road to Maracas, and the hills which framed the landscape were tinted with a soft blue mist. A mango scent mingled with the perfume of over-ripe cocoa. Every few yards, a gap in the growth offered a glimpse of a garden path sloping down the hillside in rows of chives and thyme, and from time to time, we came upon a clearing with a row of cottages with slanting roofs and tiny outhouses and, on either side of each set of front steps, a flaming ixora bush or a scatter of periwinkles to affirm the difference between a front garden and a back one. A few fowls scrabbled and clucked at the sides of the houses. We met young men and women coming down the hill on their way to the standpipe, and they greeted us so pleasantly that I remembered how an old woman I met one morning, as I walked up one of the Bathsheba hills, told me that nothing pleased her more than to see strangers enjoying her village. 'I does feel too nice,' she said, which was more eloquent and certainly more refined a welcome than the screaming banners and posters of the tourist agencies.

It began to rain, drip-drip on the leaves overhead, when we had walked for about half an hour. At first, the fall was too light to pay any attention to, no more than a staccato accompaniment to the scuffing sound of our feet among the dead leaves, and we went merrily along trying to think what life must have been like when cocoa was king. One of us wondered how long it would be before we reached the end of the track and won a view of the sea from the top of the hill near Saut d'Eau. The track wound through the cocoa, the Sunday sun came through the thick canopy of foliage and dappled the ground at our feet, all sweetness and filtered light. Then, all of a sudden, in a cloudburst of decision, the rain came down bucket a drop. The sight of a house standing by itself near the edge of the path made us decide that we were getting too wet for comfort and that the slight overhang of its roof would be a convenient shelter.

We lined ourselves off under the eaves, instinctively muting our voices so as not to draw attention to our presence. One of us had been provident enough to pack a flask of Mount Gay in his satchel and he passed it around to forestall any possible chill. As we drank, a woman called out to us to come in out of the rain. The sweetness of the patois in the voice made the invitation irresistible, and we went inside the house and were given chairs in a bare room in which a table with cups and plates under a coloured oilcloth and a tall wooden cupboard were the only other pieces of furniture, and a print of the Sacred Heart the only decoration on the walls. The woman's skin was the colour of copper, but from under a bright head-tie, her hair escaped in springy coils of grey. Her tired face brightened as she wished us good morning and reassured us that it was only a passing shower; and then she went to the window which looked out on the back yard and began to help a young man, who had his back to us and who hadn't even looked around when we entered the house, wash some dishes.

The young man was of indeterminate age. He had an oversized head which, seen from the back, gave him a grotesque appearance. He washed some tin cups and a saucepan blackened with soot, and turned them down to drain on the ledge in the window. A young girl, on the brink of nubility, passed through the room, smiled shyly, and went through the back door. We could hear her voice talking to the young man from outside. The woman whispered something to the young man after he had finished washing the cups, and he poured some clean water from a bucket into the saucepan. I took the woman to be his mother from the way she let her eyes rest on him. When he turned to face us with his large head, he had that gentle, innocent calf look which retarded children frequently have. The woman went to a wooden cupboard and took out four coffee cups and saucers decorated with a blue pattern and put them on the table. When the water in the saucepan began to boil, she said, 'How do the gentlemen like their coffee? Black?' The patois accent sang in her voice.

While the woman was making the coffee, one of us asked her whether many people went walking up the hill, but she did not catch the meaning of the question and said that we were the first she had seen this morning. No one bothered to pursue the academic question, because the coffee was ready and each of us murmured thanks as the woman handed him a demi-tasse.

The flask of Mount Gay was passed round again and we strengthened our cups.

We drank the strong black coffee very cosily with the rain drumming on the roof, but no sooner had we finished than the rain stopped. The young man grinned at us at last when he took our cups from us. We shook hands with the woman, and said goodbye. She wished us well and told us to go safely.

I cannot remember any details of the rest of that Sunday morning's events, except that we walked over damp leaves and that, occasionally, a water droplet, suspended on the tip of a cocoa or mango leaf or on the frond of a heliconia, caught the sunlight and sparkled like a jewel. I can summon up no collection of how far up the hill we reached, whether we persevered to the top, or whether we ever set eyes on the sea on the other side of the hill. The journey back down to the village centre where we had left the car has left not the faintest mark on my mind. But I have not been able these many years to put away the memory of the most aristocratic gesture of hospitality I have known. It was the very essence of hospitality, unobtrusive, expressed not in insistent invitation, but in the gentlest confidence that we would have a cup of coffee with our hostess. The superb style of the gesture was prompted by the simple and instinctive assumption that, as guests, we were bound by the same primitive convention that bound her who was our hostess, and that though the group of us might never collide again, for a few moments we had been caught in a context of mutual awareness, the same web of time, the bonds of a common humanity.

I cannot help thinking that Clem's welcome and the hospitality of the nameless woman of Paramin belong to the same family of behaviour and are, both of them, vivid articulations of the spirit which defined the city and provided me with a distinct clue to its personality.

The first meeting with Clem left a haunting impression. It was clear that I could not be content with that single visit, and I was certainly not prepared to wait for Cecil to take me round again. The more I thought about the house and the collection and the man, the less credible their existence became. The whole experience of that first visit, the Debussy in the dim light, the pinging of the wine glass, the hoarse chuckle and the pervasive smell of old furniture and books, seemed like a dream. I could have been persuaded that it had never happened. But I spoke to no one and prepared to find Clem again by myself.

One Saturday morning, with the taxi drivers crying for fares and the whole length of Marine Square crowded with shoppers and "con" men and limers, I made my way past the Cathedral of the Immaculate Conception in an attempt to find Clem's house, not from South Quay but from the Piccadilly Street Old St Joseph Road side. I had some odd idea that the house would be more easily spotted from the back. The bustle thinned out quickly beyond the statue of Columbus in Tamarind Square, and the small neighbourhood shops and parlours became more ramshackle and more intimate the further east I went. I asked a woman with her grandchild in her arms if she knew where Clem Philips lived, explaining that I would know the house if I saw it.

'Clem Philips? Clem Philips? An old man? He was a postman?'

I couldn't tell her. I didn't know. I could only describe an old man with a bald pate, very few teeth and a passion for classical music. I told her that he had a lot of records.

'Oh, I know who you mean. You have to go round the other side.'

And that was how I found that there was only one entry to Clem's street; a cul-de-sac.

I knocked and knocked and shouted, but no one was at home. The houses in the narrow street were very much alike, and I marked Clem's by the jacaranda bush in the tiny front gardens and a slanting coconut tree in the back garden whose top branches were visible over the roof; the only features to distinguish it from the other grey-painted houses which made an enclave of the area.

Eventually, I did find Clem at home one evening, and he greeted me as if we were old friends with a casualness and an absence of surprise that was very touching. I said that I was sorry that I was calling without warning and he laughed at my formal manners.

'You don't have to give me any warning, except to save yourself the trouble of coming and not finding me here. Warning? Fie upon you!'

He put me in my place and at ease at the same time. He explained that he went out every day (I got the impression that it was to a son in Belmont) for his meal, and in the afternoon he collected food for his ducks, but I should normally find him at home in the evening and I was welcome whenever I felt like dropping in. He showed me where he left the key to the front door. All I had to do was to put my hand through the jalousie and take it, open up and make myself comfortable with some music until he turned up. I did not let him know that I had made a couple of attempts to see him since my first visit with Cecil.

In the years that followed, I visited Clem regularly and came to know him well. I took a few of my friends to

meet him, but I was always careful whom I introduced
to the house and the ambience, because the better I came
to know him, the more clearly I saw how easy it was
for people to misread him; and once or twice, I was
embarrassed by the condescending manner which was
considered appropriate. And yet, although, as I say, I
knew him well, it was remarkable how little I knew of
him. Knowing him and being his friend did not at all
depend on any familiarity with the circumstances of his
life. I went abroad from time to time for longish periods: I
would write to him, send him a card and, when I returned
to Port-of-Spain, would tell him what I had seen and
enjoyed. And he would tell me what he had done, what
new piece he had acquired. But he said very little about
himself. The details of his life which he chose to share
with me were enough, he judged cannily, to satisfy the
claims of the particular relationship which he had decided
was warranted, and that judgement remains one of the
most astute and perceptive insights into the nature of
friendship that I know. Enough is enough, he understood
through his instinct and his experience, for he had the
minimum of formal schooling, that there is an area of
mutual interest, affection and concern which is available
for exploration, but beyond which lies a dominion where
trespassing is forbidden and whose privacy must be kept
inviolable.

Not that he was secretive. Not by any means. What I
learned of him, I had from his own lips. But I learned
from him too that the most certain way to be misinformed
is to seek information by direct questions. Ask no question,
he said, hear no lies; put down no molasses, catch no
flies.

We sat in the dark listening to music and Clem told
me how he came to start collecting classical records. One
of the department stores on Frederick Street was going
out of business and offered a sale of a large stock of
records, mainly of classical music on the old 78s. They

147

were virtually giving them away at twelve cents each and
he, a poor postman, was attracted. He bought one of the
old horn gramophones at a sale for next to nothing and
began, week by week, one at a time, to acquire what
was to become his passion. Imagine, he said, a record a
week, twelve cents a week, and yet there were some weeks
when he couldn't afford to buy. But old Mr Whoever was
indulgent and would save his choices for him. In any case,
how many people were interested in classical music? He
had some of the best: Roland Hayes, the young Robeson,
Caruso, some early jazz – *Ain't she sweet?*, *Mean to me*.
People thought he was mad; a postman buying records!
They couldn't understand. But, you know, he said, it's
funny, they would have understood if he had been buying
rum. The joke of it amused him. And when the electric
players came, he went straight up to Mr So and So and
told him, as man to man, 'Look, I must have something
decent to play my records on and I don't have any money.'
Mr So and So was flabbergasted at the cheekiness of it.
'No, Clem,' he said. 'You won't be able to afford one of
these.' And Clem said, 'Try me and see.' And just by
being bold-faced, he got what he wanted. 'And I paid
for it too, every cent. That's a good one, eh? But I have
a better one for you. Your humble servant don't know a
note of music. If you put a sheet of music before him as
big as the Red House, he wouldn't be able to tell one note
from another. He couldn't make a note. That's a joke for
you, eh?' And he collapsed into a chuckle of laughter at
his disability that left him weak.

But he loved music. 'I have heard every single visiting
artist since I was eighteen. Marian Anderson had water
coming from my eye. Bruce Wendell, Odnoposoff; Robeson, I went to hear him three times, and have his
autograph too. I can't complain, I have heard the best
of them and those I haven't heard in person, I have
heard on records. You can't beat that. Music, man, the
language of the gods.' Another time: 'Listen, man, what I

want with money? Money to do what with? Die and leave for somebody else to spend? Not me. You see that set of candlesticks? It was in a sale in St Clair and I say I want it, I went before the sale start to the auctioneer and I say, "Look, I am interested in those candlesticks." He asked me, "Clem, what you going to do with them old things?" He knew me well, I could have told him anything. I say, "That's none of your blasted business. I want them and I must have them." This time, the things old and looking dirty too, bad, and the old stupid man saying, "Clem, what you want with candlesticks and they have so much electric light all over the place?" The bidding start low, low, a few dollars. I didn't open my mouth. When it reached twenty dollars, hear Clem! I shout, "thirty!" and I had them bouleversé. People looking round to see who the madman was. Before you could say Jack Robinson, the auctioneer say "Going, going, gone," and I have my candlesticks. Easy so. And you know something? Who tell you that one of them white people didn't come running behind me asking if I would take a hundred dollars for the set? I tell her, "No thank you, lady!" And I come home.'

'And you see all them books inside there? I bought them at sales too, some at six cents, some at four cents, with langniappe too, you know. Believe that. Oscar Wilde, Thackeray, Sir Walter Scott, James Boswell, all them giants for a bob!'

In his bedroom, all round the high four-posted with its old style tester, piles of books reached nearly to the ceiling, copies of the Koran, scholarly Hebrew volumes, the Kama Sutra, medical encyclopedias, whatever came in the rag bag of jumble and auction. He entertained me in his room one evening when he was feeling ill with the 'flu and looking more gnome-like and mischievous than ever in his pyjamas among the bedclothes. He made me search in the bottom drawer of a high chest of drawers until I found a bottle of rum, and there was a monkey of water in the kitchen. We passed the time very companionably and it was that evening that he told me about the ducks.

The subject came up when I asked him who was looking after him. His reply was that he didn't need anyone to look after him, but his ducks were a bother. Had been for a long time. He kept a flock of ducks in his yard and every evening, by arrangement, he went to a Chinese restaurant near Park Street to collect the scraps which the Chinaman allowed him from the kitchen for the ducks' feed. I could not be sure and I never asked, but I got the impression that the arrangement involved the supply of ducks to the restaurant. However, there was some kind of falling out, and Clem was determined to put an end to the arrangement. He wasn't going to sell the ducks, eighty-four of them. He had a more direct solution, absolutely elegant in its simplicity. He was going to eat them.

'But there are eighty-four ducks, Clem. You can't eat eighty-four ducks.' I said that I thought that was going a trifle far.

'Not at one time, you dummy,' he said. 'But a duck a day; curried duck, duck soup, roast duck, duck in all ways. A duck a day till all gone.'

It was beautifully simple. It was impossible not to admire Clem.

I never knew, never bothered to try to know whether Clem had ever married or what his marital status was. Whatever it may have been, it was quite irrelevant to our friendship. He used, once in a way, to mention "the boy", but this was not often nor obsessive and when he did, it was to say, without any undertone of regret, that the boy was not much interested in any of the things he had collected. It seemed a pity, I said once, that something so lovingly and patiently created should be destroyed. But he would have none of that talk. He said that he had had his pleasure, the collection was his, and any meaning it had came from the fact that he had made it and it was his creation. When he was gone, its relevance and its value would, by definition, come to an end. He spoke without reproach or self pity. It was impossible not to admire him.

But so long as he was alive, he guarded his collection with jealous care. One of the first things he told me was that he was not a lender.

'You can come here as often as you like, and listen and look as long as you like, but don't ask me to lend you anything.' He told me what happened when he was persuaded, against all his principles, to lend his only recording of Handel's *Harmonious Blacksmith*, one of the old 78s in perfect condition.

The man whose name he mentioned was a well known Port-of-Spain figure, busy on committees, with his photograph in the newspaper, a culture vulture. He was organising some kind of soirée, Clem said, for which, for some reason, the Handel suite was essential. The man had been searching all over the town, but had been unable to find a recording of the music. Inevitably, in due course he arrived at Clem's front door. Clem, of course, said quite bluntly that he never lent any of his records and that he had no intention of doing so on this occasion. Days of pleading followed. The man was not only importunate himself, but he mobilised his friends to intercede on his behalf.

'Man,' Clem said, 'he all but cried. And he got his friends to cry too, until I was the most selfish person in the world because I refused to lend him my record.'

In the end, Clem weakened, and the man took the record, promising to guard it with the equivalent of his life and to return it promptly. Clem came as close to tears as he ever did in my presence when he told the story for he never saw the record again.

'Can you believe, John, what that man had the face to tell me when I rang him, I had to ring him, to ask for my record? Guess! The man said that he had the record on a chair and one of the children sat on it, but he was quite prepared to pay what I asked for it.

I could have killed him, I tell you, easy so, I could have killed him.'

It was a feeling with which most people would have an instant sympathy.

I believe that, for Clem, Port-of-Spain was the world. In his backyard, he grew a few anthuriums and some roses. He once kept pigeons, he told me. In his house, he had music to fill all his days. He had a few, not many, faithful friends, and all those he met remembered him and were fond of him. He did not want a great deal. I once asked him why he had never wanted to travel. Did he ever have the opportunity? Yes, he had, but was never fussy about it. For why does a man travel? He asked the question and answered it himself. To taste the food and the women of another country.

'And I have had my belly full of both right here in Port-of-Spain.'

When I heard that Clem had died, I tried to remember the last time I had seen him. It was latish one evening just before Carnival. I was visiting Port-of-Spain for a few days and dropped in on him unannounced with a friend. He was delighted to see me – we hadn't seen each other for three or four years – gave us a drink of Dubonnet and offered some music. His sight was going, and as he put the Chopin on the player, I remembered how he had impressed me several years before, the first time I had met him, with the uncanny accuracy of his fingers' selection of the Debussy record. I remembered that it had crossed my mind then that if blindness ever came, it would be no handicap, for he didn't need eyes to see what he loved. It was as if, even then, he was preparing himself to deal with what otherwise would have been a calamity.

There can never have been anyone whom it was more pleasure to visit, for no one I have known was ever so pleased to see his friends. He chuckled, he showed off, he offered his wine, his music, the whole fabric of his life for your enjoyment. To say that his friends are the richer for having known him is, for once, no more than the hard truth.

As we were about to say goodbye to him that last time, he remembered to ask my friend to sign the book. When he brought it, for some unaccountable reason, I could not remember whether I had myself signed it or whether I merely thought that I had done so. But I had. There, on the appropriate page, was my autograph – a confirmation which amused Clem to his happiest chuckles.

Till we meet in the Morning

If I had not caught the measles I should not, at six o'clock on a September afternoon just after I was eighteen, have been looking disconsolately out of our front window on a nearly empty road. And if I had not been looking out of the window, I should not have had that first sight of Charlotte riding her bicycle up the gap in the fading evening.

There I was, one moment with my head resting on the window ledge, idly contemplating the asparagus fern which grew in the garden below, and the next, staring into the eyes of the most winning and loveliest face I had ever seen. Our eyes made four, Charlotte's and mine; she smiled as if I were someone she had known but had not seen for a long time and was now glad that she had. And straightaway, I was stricken with a fever which had nothing in the world to do with my measles.

Charlotte was visiting a friend who lived up the road and who had three brothers who were, until a couple of months earlier, schoolfellows, and whose family and mine were old time friends. The gap was a virtual dead end; only the canefields lay beyond, and I could therefore wait at the window in the confident assurance that what went up the gap had, by the law of circumstance, to come back down again. And so, sure as fate, Charlotte came back down the road walking with Jerome, who was pushing her bicycle for her, chatting as excitedly as a monkey. Which drove me to the extreme of a most unreasonable jealousy.

At this distance in time, I cannot understand what came over me. In my measly state, I ran out of our front door, down the steps and out into the road where I confronted Jerome and this strange, wonderful, smiling girl I had never seen before. I had never been so bold, for girls had, until that moment, made me tongue-tied and uncomfortable unless they happened to be as familiar as my sister or my friends' sisters. And yet here I was, demanding with all the authority of a newly discovered sense of possession to be introduced. Jerome was unbelieving, taken aback by such an uncharacteristic display of aggressiveness from someone he had been accustomed to regard as acquiescent to the point of anonymity. But he introduced me.

'Charlotte,' he said, 'meet Thomas, my friend.' And then, in an attempt to take back what he had reluctantly given, he said, 'Be careful, he has measles.'

Charlotte brought her face, smiling so that the laughing lines ran deep along the sides of her cheeks, she brought her face close to mine, peering at my skin, her eyes searching my face. She put out her hand and touched my face and said, laughing, to Jerome, 'But I only see one measle.'

Jerome sulked and said nothing. Charlotte put her hands in mine and we became in an instant each other's world.

Love at first sight. Is there any other kind? I expect there is, but I was not, in the ecstasy of the weeks that followed my first holding of Charlotte's hand, the first gentle touch of her fingers against my face, disposed to regard any such question as more than barren academic humbug. I don't know, don't remember, what happened to my measle – it has faded into oblivion – but I know that, without the slightest trace of shyness, as if I were doing no more than claiming my rights, I asked Charlotte where she lived. She told me that she was spending her holidays with her grandmother and she mentioned the name of a village a couple of miles away from our own. I asked her whether I could come and see her, and she nodded and smiled again as if she had known all along that I would ask just that question, as if her riding up our gap that particular evening was precisely for the purpose of hearing that question asked.

I rode over to see Charlotte at her grandmother's the very next evening, after spending twenty-four hours in a sweat of anxiety. Her grandmother was a bony, sharp-faced 60, wrinkled as a map, with two bright, restless eyes. She shook my hand briskly.

'Are you saved? Do you know Christ as your saviour?' The questions were curt and shot at me, as if she were checking my credentials. But she did not wait for an answer.

'Charlotte,' she cried, in a sharp bark of a voice. 'A young man is here to see you.'

Had Charlotte spoken about me so soon? I liked the old girl in a moment, and although in the following few days I came to see that she did not disapprove of me, I could never get rid of the feeling that I had somehow failed by not being able to answer those first sharp questions.

Charlotte came out from the back of the house. It was only twenty-four hours since I had first and last seen her and yet, strangely, she seemed as wonderful as if I had never seen her before. She gave me a slow, intimate, between-the-two-of-us smile. Her grandmother left us.

'Till we meet in the morning,' Grandmother said, leaving me bewildered. Was it her way of letting me know that she was relying on me not to overstay the limits of propriety? Nice, I thought. Neat. But it wasn't that at all. Charlotte explained that she was referring to the morning of judgement, when the great trump would sound and all men and women would face the terrible majesty of the Almighty Judge.

'Till we meet in the morning.' I was to hear those words often in the next days, every evening, but they never grew stale; and, even now, they seem to offer a prospect which had its original delight in the promise that tomorrow I should see Charlotte again.

Faint heart ne'er won fair lady. So I had been told. That first evening after her grandmother had left us, I told Charlotte that I loved her. I had never ventured that profession before: the boys had often talked about the idea of love, but we had never come to any conclusion about what it might be and how we should know when it was present. We had agreed that, both word and reality, it was something to be afraid of. But now I had forgotten that fear, and the words came rushing out as if I knew what it meant, as if they had been there on the tip of my tongue waiting to be uttered as soon as the time was ripe.

I said, 'I love you, Charlotte.' I was standing away from her, not even holding her hand, and I could hear myself. The words sounded stern, as if they were the words of a lesson and she were my pupil and I was stressing that it was important that she should lock them in her memory and never forget them.

'I know,' she said. That was all. Simply that she knew. And I was so overcome by that stark acknowledgement that my eyes filled with tears. It was as if we were speaking according to a text which we knew by heart. I felt that I had everything I should ever want and I hoped that Charlotte would understand that I was crying because I was grateful. She did know. She rested her hand on my arm and turned her face up to me.

It is quite remarkable how often events of no particular moment in themselves flow together to become memorable or auspicious. I remember that in those early days, at the same time that Charlotte and I discovered each other, I was reading an Edgar Wallace novel, a fact in itself a saddening reminder of the passage of time. No one reads Edgar Wallace now, I suppose, and I shouldn't be at all surprised if there are literate men and women who have never heard of him. In the first chapter of this detective story, right at the beginning of the book, the author introduced two young people who had, just like Charlotte and me, discovered each other and were experiencing the wonder of first love. Between these two, the author said, there was no need for long and patient exploration . . . for them, to meet and to be met was to understand and be understood.

That was exactly how it was with Charlotte and me. I latched on to Edgar Wallace's words with all the astonished delight of the fledgling at the discovery of flight, or of the adolescent upon meeting an arrangement of words exactly appropriate to his own personal and private experience. It seemed that the world was for us, that everything we had ever seen or done before we met was no more than a preparation for our meeting. I recited poetry for her and told her stories I had forgotten, or thought I had. And she listened to what I said with a sweet sad patience as if what I was saying was wise and important.

Every evening, as soon as it was five o'clock, I jumped on my Hopper bicycle (where have all the Hoppers gone?), rode furiously over the two miles that separated us and knocked on the door of Charlotte's grandmother's house. How callous is the young lover! All he is concerned with is his own ecstasy. Nothing else matters, no one exists but his loved one and himself, and he walks around as blind to the world and as single-minded as a young puppy. Every evening, I would shake a wrinkled, bony hand, smile an empty smile and look expectantly towards the door through which my dearest Charlotte would make her appearance. Grandmother, bless her, after a few minutes, would bid me her goodbye. 'Till we meet in the morning,' and make a discreet exit, and Charlotte and I would be left together to swear love that would last beyond the grave.

It was a sweet time, those days of first love. Charlotte. She was always smiling or laughing, and she took me with her on her laughter and quiet smiles careering over the plans for our life and love together. Without a word, we had agreed that a future we did not share would be no future at all. We were as sure of that as any human beings could be sure about anything. When the old clock on its bracket against the partition struck nine and we heard the sound of a throat being cleared, we weeent through the front door, down the front steps and Charlotte on her side of the wire fence, her hands outstretched in mine, we said our reluctant goodbyes to each other, secure in the knowledge that there would be another meeting tomorrow with yet another assurance of lifelong devotion. Love was boundless and time could have no stop.

I was due to go back to work on the same day, a Monday, that Charlotte was leaving to return to her home in the country. I could not, we could not, believe that two weeks before we had not ever seen each other. Our meeting was a miracle that made us sad to think that it might never have happened but for the accident of my measles and my being at the window at the precise time of Charlotte's passing. When we said goodbye on the Saturday night, I asked Charlotte what she thought we should do the next day, our last together.

She said, 'Let's go for a walk.' I nearly burst out laughing. A walk! That was for children, walking on a Sunday afternoon. Charlotte was so simple, so childish. Yet, the childishness was touching. It showed how innocent and unspoilt she was. Her innocence, that was such an attraction for me, that made her seem so vulnerable, flattered me into a manly, protective role and made me feel responsible for her. A Sunday afternoon walk was old-fashioned and romantic, and I was touched. Going for walks was something that lovers did.

I said, 'Yes, that would be nice. Let's go for a walk. I know just where we ought to go. I'll call for you about four.'

And at four o'clock when I called for her, she was ready. Her punctuality was another flattery. A streak of powder on her cheek gave me an excuse to touch her face, I wiped the smudge with my handkerchief, a gesture of intimacy and possession and affection and concern. She smiled her slow smile, pleased by my attention. I leaned my Hopper inside the garden fence, took her hand in mine and we walked towards the main road.

I knew exactly where I was going to take her. Behind our house, a hill rose unexpectedly from the surrounding field of sour grass. It was not a hill of any great proportions: it was our sort of hill, modest, laughable compared to real hills, little more than a rising, but we called it The Hill. And, covered with scrub, wild flowers and dunks trees, it provided children with a thrill of adventure to clamber up the winding rocky paths on one side, and a sense of achievement to stand on the top and look down upon the town over the houses of the well-to-do folk and pick out the landmarks; the schools, the public buildings, the cathedral and the blue bay with the masts of schooners in the foreground and, beyond, in the outer basin of the harbour, a man-of-war riding heavily at anchor.

As small, wild children, my friends and I had flown kites from this hill and when, inevitably, a kite string broke, we watched the delicate thing we had laboured to make pretty sail away in the wind with its tail writhing like a snake over the housetops as it fell, fell and then disappeared in a far garden beyond hope of rescue. But, distressing though the sight of our loved kite sailing away from us was, there was always consolation in the knowledge that its loss would provide us with an opportunity to show our skill, and that tomorrow we would make another and a prettier kite.

Charlotte and I walked past the houses with their tidy gardens and beware-of-the-dog signs on their gates. I showed off by telling her stories about the characters who lived in the houses and the games we used to play with the watchman on the plantation, whose canefields ran right down to the garden of the last house in the row. We walked slowly, hand in hand, trying to make the time last longer. Charlotte had a frangipani flower in her hair, which was brushed and gleaming, and tiny drops of perspiration beaded her brow and the tip of her nose. I had never seen her prettier.

The Hill was busy with little children playing hide and whoop in the bushes, their antics watched superciliously by the bigger ones who considered themselves past the stage of childish games. At the top of The Hill, one or two couples pointed out the landmarks of the town, and when we reached the top, we sat on a large boulder and I showed Charlotte where our house was and where, behind a clump of mahogany, her grandmother's house was hidden. Below us and far away to the right, the country spread out in mounds and swells of green, and the wonder of it, so far away and yet so near, made me feel that I could take two strides across the country and have it soft as a carpet under my feet.

I felt that I was seeing the landscape for the very first time; the fields gently rolling like the hummocks of gentle breasts, homely, maternal, smooth, rounded, without harshness or angles or drama in them, but patient and sustaining as if they would last forever to feed our eyes and nourish our bodies. I had my arm around Charlotte's waist and turned to her, looking down to find her eyes looking up into mine, waiting for me to say something to her, to let her into a secret I had discovered. We kissed lightly, a frightened, adolescent brush of the lips with as little passion as a punctuation mark, a comma perhaps, unnecessary except to give a pause, but at the same time an assurance that the sentence which was in progress had not come to an end.

I was sure that, with my arm around her waist, she had seen what I had seen in the promise that lay in the green, tidy arrangement of the fields and the hills sloping over to the horizon with rows of palm trees like caravans of camels, one behind the other, making their way unendingly across an infinity. I said, for the millionth time, 'I love you, Charlotte.' But the words sounded as

original as if I had made them up that very moment and
no one but myself had ever used them before.

And Charlotte said, as she had said before, 'I know.'
And with her slender, warm, girl's body so close to me,
her head barely reaching my shoulder, I understood that
acknowledgement to be her way of saying that she loved
me too. On our way down the other side of the hill, we
stopped and lay on the grass. The sky was high and deep;
the more you looked at it, the farther away it seemed, and
looking at it made the senses giddy and I felt the same
way as I did when I looked at the house in the picture in
Charlotte's grandmother's drawing room, the green house
we planned to live in on the bank of a stream which would
have on its wall a picture of another identical house which
would have on its wall a picture of another identical house
– an infinite succession too bewildering to contemplate.

My mother was still up and awake when I got home
and pushed the Hopper through our front door. She
was sitting under the light in the drawing room, her
spectacles falling down her nose as she worked on a
piece of embroidery. She had a passion for needlework
and spent hours every day working on the most intricate
designs. But for her to be working late on a Sunday night
meant that she had a deadline to meet, perhaps a present
for one of her friends who was going away.

I said, 'Hello, Mum.'

She did not answer. Her head stayed buried in the work
she was doing. I could tell by the pout of her mouth that
she was angry.

She asked me, 'Where have you been all night?'

'All night? It isn't even ten o'clock yet.' What was she
talking about? She had never quarrelled with me for
coming in late.

'Don't argue with me. D'you think you are a man? I
asked you, where have you been?'

She threw her embroidery from her in a temper and
looked at me full in the face. Her eyes travelled my whole

length from head to toe in a slow, accusing survey. It was as if she had never seen me before and was taking a careful inventory, as a mother does, to make sure that there are no deformities or uglinesses of limbs or organs in the naked new child to which she has just given birth.

'I went to see Charlotte,' I said.

'Charlotte?' My mother spoke the name as if it was completely new and strange to her, the pretended ignorance meant to be a rebuke. But why should she pretend that this was the first time she was hearing Charlotte's name? I had brought Charlotte home to see her, and she had made her welcome, given her tea and little sweet biscuits and a present of a box of handkerchiefs, hugged her and shown her around our little back garden of beans and parsley and made much of her. So what was she up to now? I was confused. I heard her voice again.

'Where did you go this evening?'

I told her that Charlotte and I had gone for a walk up The Hill.

'Up The Hill?' She sounded horrified as if we had committed the most outrageous of crimes. I was startled into fear, much as if she had caught me in some furtive mischief.

'And what were the two of you doing up The Hill?' It was an ominous sounding question. She did not wait for an answer.

'I never did like that ugly girl,' she said. 'I could see from the very first time I set eyes on her that she was no good.'

The venomous angry words were like a blow in my face. She had been so kind and welcoming to Charlotte, asking questions about her school and her parents. It was through these questions, which I myself had never thought of asking, that I had learnt that Charlotte was an orphan, that she lived with an aunt, her mother's sister, and that she had an older brother who lived in the States. I was sure that my mother liked Charlotte. Now I was hearing that it was quite the opposite. Charlotte had said, more than once, how much she liked my mother. I did not know what to say or do. My mother looked me up and down.

'What's that on your trousers?' She barked the question in a voice shrill with rage. I followed her eyes to their tour of inspection and, looking down, saw the grass burrs, the tiny "sweethearts" stuck to my trouser legs. Her eyes accused me and frightened me with the anger I saw in them.

'You think you are a man?' There was no answer that I could give.

'Do you think you are a man, lying in the grass and walking in this house at all hours of the night? And you have the face to tell me to my face that you went up The Hill with . . . with . . .' She stammered as she searched for a word terrible enough for Charlotte.

'With . . . a . . . woman!' She screamed the words in a hysteria of condemnation, as if the namelessness of the sexual identity was the most devastating insult she could think of.

'Go into my room,' she shouted at me. 'Go into that room and strip yourself naked, as naked as you were born, you hear, and wait till I come to you. You are not a man and I will show you you are not a man in this house.'

The situation had become ridiculous and I felt suddenly like laughing. A man like me, I thought, stripping naked like a little pickney, baring my backside for a beating from my mother. It was funny, in a way. But it wasn't, really. I began to feel the slow spread of a strange terror in my nerves, the same sensation which used to overcome me when I stood at the edge of the well in the cane field behind our house and looked down its unfathomable depths. Terror and a tingling fascination at the danger of falling. I could feel the sensation in my feet, in my toes, that despairing resignation which accompanies the fall through space of dreams, the end to which my mother's anger and dismay were consigning me.

It wasn't funny at all. Whatever happened, my mother and I had reached a critical point in our understanding of each other, a kind of parting in our ways, the end of a phase. After this confrontation, whatever happened, we should never be the same to each other again. I felt like crying for the loss of my childhood, the loss of all the comfort and cosiness of being a child, the loss of my mother against whom, at the insistence of some strangely irresistible call, I had to turn my back. I turned away from my mother and went into her room and took off all my clothes.

In my mother's tiny room, where she had surrounded herself in the loneliness of her widowhood with a mass of trinkets and old photographs, calendar pictures on the four walls – a clutter of "things", acquisitions of a lifetime, faded bits and pieces, little boxes, glass trays, lumps of coral that must have once caught her fancy, long stemmed vases that must once have been pretty, each piece a memory of a time, a collision, a long past delight, in my mother's tiny room I stood naked. Naked as I was at birth before the mirror which was too small to accommodate the length of my body. I stood like a man waiting for the execution of a sentence of death, but I was conscious as I inspected the reflection of my body of a satisfaction I had never before experienced.

My body was lean and hard and lithe and I was not ashamed of it. The sight of my body in the mirror took my thoughts and dispelled my apprehension: suddenly, I was a man and I knew that my mother could not harm me. I was beyond her will; and when she pushed the door, she caught me gazing like Narcissus at my reflection in the old mirror.

Our eyes caught each other's. Hers were tired and puzzled, her face lined and frightened as if the sight of my nakedness terrified her. Standing before her in my nakedness, far from ashamed, in fact, conscious of a kind of boasting, aware that my youthful, vigorous body was a flaunted reproach to her age. I felt a flood of pity of her, beyond her power. She held me in her gaze and then burst into uncontrollable tears. And a lump of love and agony rose in my throat.

My mother put her hands on my naked shoulders, reaching up to touch me, and spoke so softly that I could barely hear the words.

She said, 'Put on your clothes.' And she ran from the room, yielding her ground, defeated, weeping.

In the dark of my room, I heard through the thin wooden partition the stifled sounds of my mother's sobs but my only thought was whether Charlotte was ugly. How could she be? I thought of her face, her smile, the deep runnels of the laughing lines, the arch of her eyebrows. How could anyone find her ugly when she seemed so beautiful to me? I went to sleep with her face on my mind, seeing the tiny beads of perspiration on her nose and brow, the languid grace of her body in the crook of my arm. My mother was sobbing but I heard her from far away, for she was in another world, remote from the one I inhabited.

I went back to work at the end of my sick leave, my solitary measle cured by love. On the morning of my return to the office, I learned that I had been transferred in my absence and I got my orders to report immediately to another department. The transfer involved no more dislocation than the crossing of a narrow street, and in a few minutes I was introducing myself to a new set of colleagues, all of whom were considerably older than I was, men to my callow, hairless youth.

Among this lot was a man to whom I took an instant dislike. Although I had heard his name, I had never seen him at close range before, but our two bloods did not take. As certainly as I had known a couple of weeks before that Charlotte was for me, I knew that morning that Arthur Corben and I would not set horses.

The first source of annoyance was the way the man spelled his name. Everyone I knew with his surname spelled it Corbin, but not he, not Mr Arthur, who had to be special. I heard around the office that he changed the spelling when he began to play cricket for the island.

But what aggravated my dislike was the fact that Arthur was extremely handsome. And he knew it. He had the athletic build of the typical West Indian fast bowler that he was – he was a senior member of the island team and something of a popular hero – and to see him swaggering, broad-shouldered and slim-hipped around the office with his cricket club tie hanging loose from his collar and a cigarette hanging loose from his lips, was a constant irritation. He was boisterous; he boasted about the number of wickets and the number of women he had captured in the weekend matches. On the afternoons he was going to the nets, he changed into his cricket things in the office, clattering about in his boots with the laces untied, showing off a vulgar, aggressive masculinity.

He had travelled much more than the rest of us in the office, most of whom had never set foot outside our tiny island, and he was an authority on everything, from Carnival in Trinidad and mountain chicken in Dominica to ackee and salt-fish in Jamaica and pubs in the north of England. Everybody in the office, especially the girls, that is everybody but myself, hung on his words, every one of them, every single syllable of every one of them a pearl of wit and wisdom. I had known show-offs at school, but I had never been so close to one of them as I was now. It was as much as I could do to be civil to him, and day after day I suffered an almost physical revulsion to his presence. My dislike was so instinctive that I began to be afraid and I thought of asking to be moved to some other office. But I did not, in the end, have to.

Charlotte wrote me her first letter at the beginning of
October, soon after she had settled back in school. I got
home one evening to find the envelope with the rounded
schoolgirl script placed obtrusively on the piano. The
letter was full of love and remembrances, and between
the pages she had pressed the petals of a hibiscus flower,
a golden butter colour with a flush of scarlet in the centre.
I wrote page after page in reply, words I did not know I
knew, so powerful is love to improve the vocabulary.

She wrote again in a week. She was coming down to
spend Christmas with her grandmother and we should
be happy together. I had been hoping that she would ask
me to come up to see her one weekend but she did not,
and I had the thought that she did not want me to meet
her aunt.

But her letter was warm and sweet. She did not write of
love but she remembered everything we said, everything
we did, and her recounting of our evenings together
was more touching than any protestation. Her letter was
simple and all the more affecting for that. She asked me
if I had gone to see her grandmother since she left, if I
remembered the green house by the stream and how we
had decided to furnish it and how we had made up a fancy
that we should have a picture exactly like the original, so
that in our house there would be another house in which
there would be another house. Our heads had gone wild
with the imagination. And, begging me not to write her
again, to wait for Christmas, she signed her letter. 'Till we
meet in the morning, Your Charlotte.'

During the first week of November, a list began to
make the rounds of the office. When it reached me, I
saw that it was for a subscription for a wedding present
for Arthur Corben. Almost everyone in the office had
put his name down for some money to be paid up at
the end of the month. I read down the list. I signed
my name to show that I had seen it and put a dash
in the column under "Amount". And that simple action

was sufficient to make sure that I heard nothing more about Arthur Corben's wedding. I could tell from the exchanges I overheard that it was to be a big wedding, a cricketer's wedding, with plans for the couple to walk under an arch of cricket bats as they left the church; but I had no interest in it and, as I asked no questions, I heard nothing.

I went to see Charlotte's grandmother early in December. I had taken Charlotte at her word and not written to her, but I was in a fret for news about her, when she was coming down, how she was. Grandmother was glad to see me, rebuked me amiably for not coming to see her in all the past weeks. She asked me if I had heard from Charlotte, and when I told her that Charlotte had asked me not to write, she said that she hoped I understood how it was with young girls sometimes. I asked her whether she knew when Charlotte was coming down for Christmas.

'She is coming down?' She seemed surprised to hear. But she went on.

'Anyway, Charlotte knows very well that she can come whenever she wants to. She might just turn up, just like that.' And she snapped her fingers to indicate suddenness and an impromptu appearance.

I looked at the picture of the green house, our green house by the river while Grandmother prattled. She thought Charlotte and I would make a tidy pair. Tidy? I thought. That's an odd word to use for a pair, a couple. But Grandmother was going on. Charlotte was a good girl and she hoped, archly I thought, that her husband, whoever he was, might be, would take good care of her.

I rose, stretched out my hand and said that I had to be running.

'So soon?' Grandmother asked. 'But you have only just come,' she said.

I said, 'Till we meet in the morning,' and she smiled, pleased by the quotation.

She said, 'Till we meet in the morning.' And I went down the steps, took my Hopper from its place beside the wire fence and went away.

Arthur Corben's wedding took place the week before Christmas, on a Saturday, and on the Monday morning the office buzzed with stories and comments on how the bride looked and the women's dresses. There were one or two suggestions that Arthur might have done better, that the bride was plainish and that she would need luck to cope with Arthur. The honeymoon was being spent in New York where they both had relatives living.

In the morning newspaper, there was a picture of the happy couple smiling as they walked under an arch of cricket bats. Charlotte was leaning on Arthur's arm and their gloved fingers were entwined.

But I must cut a long and painful story short. Although I must admit that telling it was not as half as painful as I had so long thought it would be, I should never have bothered to tell it at all if I had not this morning met a young man: Charlotte's son.

At one time, I had thought that a career in the Civil Service was not for me, that it was too dull; and I used all the fancy words I heard others using to describe it. That there was no scope in the service for intelligence and initiative, that it attracted only the mediocre and the safe and unambitious. But I have stayed. It has not been an exciting career, not by any means, but it has its rewards, the greatest of which is that its very dullness, the very modesty of its demands upon what little spark of brightness I left school with, helped me to come to terms with myself after I saw Charlotte leaning on Arthur Corben's arm.

Now, after 40 years, I believe that I stayed because, after I lost Charlotte (I never saw her again), I lost the heart for any challenge. It was as if someone had turned off a switch and disconnected me from my power supply and though, somehow, I could go through the motions of living, I was

170

not really connected to life. But who was to know that but myself? And even I was unaware for most of the time.

Yesterday morning, the chief clerk of the department knocked on my door (I have a modicum of authority now) and, mumbling a name, shepherded in a young man who was joining the staff. This is one of the modern innovations of personnel management. In my day, you went into your new surroundings and made yourself as inconspicuously at home as possible. Someone would put a book or a sheaf of forms or a file in your hand, show you where you were to sit and tell you briefly what you were expected to do and when. There was no such fancy etiquette as introducing you around or pretending that you were a vitally important member of the team, because you knew and everyone else knew that you were not.

But things are different in this day and age, and the handsome youngster who sat before me, smiling and confident, had no misgivings about the genuineness of his welcome. It is possible that he really did believe the chief clerk when he told him that we were all one happy and contented family in the office. The young are unbelievably naive.

Nevertheless, I went through the routine to which I had become used and which I was coming to believe had its usefulness: at least it did no harm, as far as I could see. I told the young man that I was, we all were, happy that he was joining us, that I thought he would enjoy the work and the atmosphere, and that I hoped he would stay with us. I asked him where he had gone to school, what his best subjects were, did he play games and what, if any, were his hobbies? Did he have any brothers or sisters? His answers were clear and short, he was by no means shy, but I suspected that he realised that I had no real interest in him.

No, he played no games. His interest was music. He was an only child, an orphan. He spoke with a cynical directness which made me like him. I asked him his name and he smiled to remind me that I had already been told.

'Thomas Corben,' he said. 'With an "e".' He was careful to make the point. He smiled and I knew straight away who he was.

I said, 'My name is Thomas too.' And then, quickly, 'You said you were an orphan.' I hoped I did not sound too interested.

'I never knew my mother at all. She died when I was born.'

'I'm sorry,' I said.

To let him know that we had come to the end of the interview, I told him that I hoped he would feel free to come in to see me if and when he had any problems. He got up from his chair and put out his hand. As I shook his hands, some compulsion made me speak.

'Till we meet in the morning,' I said.

He gave me a startled look. 'My mother used to say that. At least, my father told me so.'

'Years ago, when I was a boy,' I said, 'it used to be a fairly common way of saying goodbye.'

The Light on the Sea

Two elderly women were sitting in the room with their backs to the sea when I stepped through the front door. They were sitting at opposite ends of the room, which was large enough, but looked even larger because it was so sparsely furnished: three or four chairs in dully grey upholstery and a table or two, but no flowers on them and no pictures on the walls. I said, 'Good Morning,' and they looked in my direction, blinking but not speaking. I guessed that they could not make me out with my figure silhouetted against the bright light of the doorway and they must have been a trifle alarmed at my sudden appearance. I stepped further into the room and then they spoke, both of them together and both of them pleasantly, as if they were glad to see me, although they had never seen me before.

I asked whether there was a Mr Farley in the house and they both shook their heads and looked as if they were sorry for my sake that there was no Mr Farley to offer me. Then one of them said that, perhaps if I went downstairs, someone might be able to tell me, because the truth was that they didn't really know the names of all the guests. Both of them brightened up at this and one of them got out of her chair to show me where the staircase was. I told her that she needn't have bothered, but she came with me all the same, anxious to help.

At the bottom of the stairs, an old man, gaunt, bony-faced, with thin white hair, was sitting at a small table which was covered with a check tablecloth frayed at the edges. A small yellow plastic bowl was before him and he was staring at its contents with an expression of disgust amounting to revulsion. With a silver teaspoon, he began to stir an egg yolk which had separated from its accompanying white, and he let the yellow viscous liquid drip off the spoon back into the bowl and emitted a series of heavy, forlorn sighs. He was quite unaware of my presence and paid not the slightest attention to me. Opposite the table, a door opened on a kitchen, and as I pushed my head inside the room, a woman in a blue apron looked up from what she was doing and I asked her whether she had a Mr Farley living there. She wiped her hands in her apron and told me that she would go to let him know that he had a visitor.

The white-haired old man at the table was still sighing and stirring the yellow mess in his bowl while I waited. Another woman, whom I had not seen before, came out of the kitchen and stopped by the old man's table and asked him, solicitously, I thought, whether there was something wrong with his egg. The question irritated him and it was clear that his irritation puzzled the woman. There was nothing wrong with the egg, so far as she could see. And, indeed, from where I stood, the egg, as an egg, seemed perfectly good. But what the woman could not understand was that the old man's disgust had nothing to do with the egg, as an egg.

'Oh, my God,' he half-muttered, half-whispered. 'Look at this.' He rapped the plastic bowl with his spoon and then tilted it as if he would empty it of its yellow contents. 'But look at this, couldn't you . . .?' But words failed him, and with something like a mixture of resolve and resignation, he plunged the spoon into the bowl and raised it to his mouth. But his hand was trembling and the spoon, when it reached his mouth, was empty. And still the woman was watching him, concerned and, it seemed to me, anxious to help, could not understand what was wrong.

Mr Farley came forward to see me. He was wearing a scarlet dressing gown and deep red carpet slippers, and he smiled broadly when I moved out of the light of the doorway and he was able to see me. I had taken some fruit for him, a hand of bananas, a pawpaw and a shaddock, and when he took the bag from me, he smiled even more. He sat in a chair beside the bed and motioned me to make myself comfortable on the bed.

'I am so glad to see you,' he said.

I told him that I had been wondering how he was getting on. I had heard only a few days before that he had gone into the home.

'I am as well as an old man can be,' he said, and grinned broadly.

I had known Mr Farley ever since I was a child; he had taught me in my first class at the elementary school and I was fond of him in a pitying sort of way. He was not a good teacher of small boys: he could not keep them in order and did not really try to, and I used to feel sorry for him when the boys teased him by asking silly questions which he took seriously and to which he always tried to give considered replies. I never understood how he could not see through the questions. He never lost his temper and I used often to be angry with him, because he didn't seem to see how ineffectual he was.

It did not surprise me that Mr Farley never succeeded in his career, never became talked about but always remained a kind of butt, outside the swim of things, a harmless figure of fun. Until one evening, at his invitation, some of us who had already graduated from his class, went to his house to look at his pictures.

He lived near our school in an old house set back from the main road to town and behind what seemed to us a thick forest of trees – breadfruit, sugar apple, hog plum, soursop. The possibilities of such a house and such a forest were enormous to us, and Mr Farley immediately went up in our estimation.

That afternoon we sat around a room full of dark mahogany furniture – what-not, an old sideboard with a lion's head carved on its back panel and an assortment of rocking chairs. An old oil lamp stood on the sideboard.

The rooms smelt of dust and mildew, but it was cosy. Mr Farley gave us lemonade and sweet biscuits, and when we had finished eating, he brought some of his pictures for us to look at: water colours and a few oils and some sketches in ink.

I did not like the sketches and remember thinking that they were childish; the outlines were weak. But the water colours were like Mr Farley himself, muted and shy. Some of them were of the sea, which he made look like an inland lake of quiet dappled water. He took us into a dark cellar under the house where hundreds of canvases were stacked carelessly on the floor around the walls. It was too dark to see them very clearly, but many of them looked as if they consisted only of shapes randomly arranged. In a way, they were frightening, like creatures bred of the dark shadows of the cellar and never seeing the light. I was glad to escape back up the stairs and into the relative brightness of the parlour.

Now, as I sat on his bed, I thought: how like a child he is! He was babbling with excitement at being visited, like a child given a present. I asked him if he remembered the afternoon when a group of us visited him and he showed us his pictures, but he had forgotten. It was too long ago, I suppose. And I asked him if he still painted and what had become of the pictures. Had he sold them?

'Oh,' he said, 'I left them behind at the house when I came here.' He dismissed them as if they were part of something he had discarded and would prefer to forget; there had been so many pictures in the cellar, hundreds of them, and I was tempted to ask him to let me go and look at them. Who could tell? There might be a masterpiece lurking in that gloom, waiting to be discovered. I could not believe that he had left them behind, just like that. I asked him what he planned to do with them.

'Nothing,' he said. 'They weren't any good.' He did not sound regretful but, rather, relieved, as if he had rid himself of a great, unbearable burden at last.

176

I asked him, 'Did you think when you were young, that you would ever come to a life without painting – a canvas and brushes and paints?'

He answered simply. 'It was always only a hope, never a conviction. But hope sustained until . . .' His voice trailed away as if he no longer remembered the sequence of events.

The bare, poorly-furnished room was without books or pictures, uncurtained, with only a single window through which the morning sunlight poured bright and undiluted, a spare bed across the width of the room in a far corner, no flowers and the ceiling stained brown with water from the floor above. Yet, while I was saddened by the bare and loveless look of the room and the lonely figures of the other members of the household, the two old women in the living room and the gaunt man in the kitchen sighing over his egg as he recalled better days, as I thought about the terrible loneliness to which old age had sentenced them, I had to accept that Mr Farley was cheerful. Perhaps it was because he had never had a family; he had always been lonely and this state was not new to him. He was smiling when he began to speak.

'All those pictures,' he said, 'and, believe me, I never felt as if I had ever finished a single one of them. There was always something to be done to complete every one. So I never had any satisfaction. I would put it aside, meaning to go back and finish it, but I was never able to. Another picture would come to mind and crowd the last effort and failure out, and I never looked at that last one again; I was never able to remember what I wanted to paint.'

'It must have been like a nightmare,' I said, 'or a series of nightmares, never being able to recall the vision that started the picture.'

'Frustration it was, and confusion. That's what it was. I am glad for this peace now.' And he looked around the room, the bare and cheerless room, like a child welcoming an open space where he could run and romp.

'How do you spend your time now?' It was, all of a sudden, important for me to know.

'I look at the sea,' he said, so solemnly that I thought he was making fun of the question. But he wasn't.

'You know,' he said, 'I never knew what light was. All those years behind those trees in that dark house. The light used to trickle through the leaves, only trickle, never flow. Mark you, I used to like it, I didn't complain. I thought the gloom was pleasant. But I never knew what light was.'

'And how did you come to find out, to see the light?' I asked.

'I was lucky. When my sister died, there was no one to look after things; I had never learned to cook. My friend told me about this place. The moment I saw it, with the light on the sea, I knew that I was not going back to that dark house.'

'So you just upped and left your pictures and the furniture and everything?'

'It was easy and, besides, what was there to wait for? They look after me very well here, the girls are kind and they leave me alone, which is a kindness. Do you understand how being left alone can be a real kindness? And, now, look, you have come to see me. You never came to the old house.'

'Don't you feel lonely here?'

'No, not lonelier than I have always felt. I have never been what you could call gregarious. And I never get tired of looking at the sea.'

He laughed, and I said goodbye and told him that I would come soon to see him again.

'When you came,' he said, 'I was going to have a shower.' He clutched his dressing gown with a dramatic gesture, like Gielgud clutching his toga in Julius Caesar. I never thought that he had such panache in his make-up. As he spoke, he was making his way to the bathroom, and by the time I reached the door and looked back to see what he was doing, he had already put me out of his mind.

When I stepped outside the front door, I found one of the old ladies pulling dry yellow leaves off a hibiscus bush in the untidy garden. She was so intent on what she was doing that she did not even reply when I said goodbye.

The bright Sunday morning glistened and the sea sparkled vast and wide and flat to the horizon.

Prospect

Returning to Prospect was as refreshing as being reborn. You can have no idea what it was like to be once more on the scene of one's earliest and therefore one's most genuine triumphs. If I live to be a hundred, there will never be a sweeter moment than when, having flung my suitcase down on the bed in my old room and taken off my shoes, I went out on to the front verandah where, as a small boy . . .

One somnolent Sunday afternoon, a small boy, lying on the floor of the verandah of his grandparents' house while they rocked and dozed after their midday meal, was a shy, furtive and frightened witness to what he could only describe as "something" between his grandfather and his Gran. The thing that happened – although "happened" is perhaps too vulgarly positive, too gross a word to apply to what took place, what came to pass in a few moments that Sunday afternoon – was as muted as a murmur, no more stressed than a toneless whisper. And yet, to the small boy lying on his belly on the floor, it was an explosion more terrifying in its implications than if these two beloved grandparents had come to blows and angry words in the presence of their grandson.

The boy had his head stuck through the verandah rails so that he could catch the Atlantic breeze on his face. The breeze was making him sleepy, and he was thinking of nothing more important than that it would soon be time for the first fishing boats to be rounding the point on their way home to the bay at the bottom of the cliff that fell away below the verandah. And then, suddenly, with no more warning than a thunder clap out of a clear blue sky, the afternoon turned heavy and bodeful with hurt and despair. One moment, all was drowsy afternoon peace, three people half dozing, content in their nearness to each other, asking no questions because there were none to be asked; and the next, the air was sharp and jangling with discord, and the idle-minded boy lying on the floor felt suddenly as if, having bitten through the sour flesh of an unripe mango, all his teeth had been set on edge.

What astonished the boy was that there was no shocking revelation, no quarrel, no temper tantrum, not even a difference of opinion. All that happened, or seemed to, was that his grandfather spoke to himself. Perhaps his mind had caught itself in a reverie, and he had forgotten that he was sitting with his wife and his grandson within earshot on his front verandah, with the wind on his face, after his Sunday dinner. He spoke in the tone of voice of one stating a fact, not at all as if he had made any discovery nor as if he were whispering a secret he did not wish to share with his wife nor with the little boy lying on the floor with his face to the wind. All that happened was that his grandfather, looking out to sea, murmured almost inaudibly to himself.

'I always wanted to go to Africa,' he said. And the voice trailed off, as if the old but unforgotten dream was too fragile, too tenuous for loud or emphatic utterance.

But the boy understood well enough that nothing his grandfather said would be too soft or whispered for his grandmother to overhear, no gesture too fleeting, no smile or grimace or texture of glance so innocuous as to escape his Gran's affectionate attention. She was out of her doze in a cat's flash, her eyes as wide and wondering as a child's, the sea breeze ruffling the silver hair under her bonnet, and she fixed a searching, startled look on the old man. But he was not even looking at her. Unaware of any disturbance in the pool which was just a moment before as placid as porridge in a breakfast bowl, he went on gazing beyond the horizon to Africa, not dreaming that he had done more than spoken a harmless dream too old now to be satisfied. Gran looked alarmed, the boy thought, as if she had suddenly been given some news for which she had not been prepared and it had overwhelmed her. Lying there on the floor, he felt his own innocence and the bliss of being with his grandparents ambushed by a doubt and a dismay that he had never felt before. His belly grew tight with a strange fear, and he had the same feeling of loss and disappointment which always came over him when a Christmas balloon collapsed in his hand in a hiss of air.

The current of tension flowed along the look his grandmother sent across to his grandfather who, when it touched him, looked sharply around and traced it to its source. From where the boy lay on the floor, the angle of his anxious glance had the effect of foreshortening his grandfather's bony face, indenting even more the already hollow temples and sunken cheeks. Looking upwards past a familiarly stern but not unkind thrust of jaw, the boy guessed that the eyes he could not see were shadowed with alarm as they searched his grandmother's face. But whatever his eyes may have seen, his grandfather said nothing. He turned his gaze back to the sea stretching beyond the verandah rail to Africa and it occurred to the boy, stunned and confused as he was by the traffic of glances and looks whose meaning he could not quite understand, that his grandfather was not aware that he had said anything to alarm anyone.

The boy saw his grandfather look across at this grandmother again, quickly this time, but the look was not acknowledged nor returned, although the boy knew by instinct that his grandmother would have felt the old man's eyes on her. She knew well enough, the boy was sure, that the old man was ransacking his mind to unravel the mystery of his offence. Goose pimples rose on the boy's skin and he wanted, for no reason that he could fathom, to bury his head in his grandmother's lap and cry. If ease and peace could be destroyed so easily, here one moment, gone the next, without malice or intent, then he was not safe from danger and loneliness.

The moment she opened her mouth, the boy knew that his grandmother was angry. She tried her best, he could tell, to compose her voice, to make it sound casual and open, but she did not succeed. The words, when she spoke, came out metallic, dry. Her anger was only very thinly camouflaged by the falsetto.

'But, Sampeter,' she said, 'you have never said that before. In all these fifty-something years, I have never heard you say that you had a yearning for Africa.'

The "Sampeter" was mocking, formal. Not Matthew nor even the "Dads" which sometimes came into use. "Sampeter" harked back to the amusing (to the boy) formality of their courting days, of which they had told him endless stories, back to the days when they were still separate persons. Now, after fifty-something years, they were separate again. The thought frightened the boy: if his grandfather and his grandmother did not exist as a single person, then where was he?

It was agony to the boy to hear his grandmother speak as if she had been betrayed, as if the years of love and children and suffering and his own existence itself were now denied by the unearthing of a long buried wish. For some unknown reason, his grandfather had kept this desire hidden all through the years, but was it too much to expect his grandmother to stifle her resentment that, although they had shared so much, she had not been asked nor allowed to share this dream, however impossible it may have been to realise? The boy was alarmed at the daring of his own question, frightened by the possibility it revealed that he might be taking sides. He waited for his grandfather to speak again. The early fishing boats were coming into shore and he watched them ploughing heavily through the water without thinking of them. He stole a glance at his grandmother. Her face was set, but her eyes held no look of anger or self pity. And it came to him that she had not spoken in anger nor rebuke nor even appeal, but only with the hard neutrality of her realisation that, even after a lifetime of being together, it was possible for two people to exist in separation from each other. Young as he was, he could understand that it had nothing to do with love or respect or affection or trust when his grandfather spoke again, his eyes still fixed on the far horizon.

'It just never came to me,' he said, 'to say anything before now. It just never came to me. And even now, I don't know why I spoke about it.'

He sounded puzzled. Why, in all these years, had he never mentioned such a simple, impossible thing as setting eyes on Africa? It was such a tiny thing, would have cost so little to say and yet he had not said it.

And the little boy lying on the floor with the trade wind on his face understood that even if his grandfather and grandmother lived for a hundred years together, there would still, at the end, be some things that it would not occur to them to say to each other. There would always be undisclosed privacies.